"Well, honey, it was just a matter of time. When they didn't find her those first few weeks, I knew she wasn't coming back. It's just a shame, she was such a beautiful girl. That blond hair...and you two were so close."

A blinding ribbbon of pain shot through my chest, punching the air out of my lungs. Memories, frozen in time like snapshots, flashed behind my closed eyelids. Kissing Natalie, our eyes open, our mouths firmly, innocently closed; holding her butter-soft hand...I found myself confessing, "I loved her."

Mom kept tidying. "Well of course you did. You were like sisters, we couldn't pry you two apart." She started busily drying a copper mold that was shaped like a rooster.

"No, Mom. I mean I *really* loved her."

She Died Twice

by Jessica Lauren

New Victoria Publishers Inc.

Published by New Victoria Publishers
P.O. Box 27 Norwich, Vermont

Cover photographs by Matthew Lamperti

ISBN 0-934678-34-0

Library of Congress Cataloging-in-Publication Data

Lauren, Jessica, 1965-
    She died twice / by Jessica Lauren.
        p.   cm.
    ISBN 0-934678-34-0 (pb.) : $8.95
    I. Title.
PS3562.A8416S44   1991
813'.54--dc20

91-1055
CIP

For Tiffany—

who is teaching me how to trust again.

Last night

I dreamed

I told you things

I've never told anyone.

j/1980

Chapter 1

It was so quiet. The bottom of the ravine lay completely in shadow, cold. High up, a fitful breeze sifted through the eucalyptus trees. A dry sound, like shuffling paper, it made the leaves tinkle together.

I was trying not to slip and fall. My feet, buckled into brown leather sandals, uncertainly picked their way over the creek bed. There wasn't any water in the creek—there never was—just a layer of polished grey stones, smooth and settled. They were so close together you had to use a stick to pry one out and see what was underneath. Natalie always did that. I never wanted to know what was underneath.

I didn't look up until I got to the bottom of the terrace. The terrace, that's what we called it, but it was really a sort of earthdam. When they built the townhouse complex, they paved the ground all the way up to the edge of the ravine, and to keep the sloping, rocky ground from eroding, they sank these huge concrete slabs into the hillside. Layer after layer, with about two feet of red clay earth showing in between. Every fifteen feet or so, a leaning vertical column held the slabs in place. It looked like a staircase for giants. Sometimes, Natalie and I pretended there was a golden castle at the top, and if we could make it all the way up, we'd become princesses and live happily ever after. But we grew out of that. Natalie started calling the steps 'the terrace' after we learned about Japanese hill farming in school. She liked the word 'terrace'—she said it made her think of lace and rose petals.

The terrace was only about thirty feet high, but from below, it looked much higher. I hated it. I hated climbing up it. But Natalie and I spent hours there every day. She always went up first, so I wouldn't be scared. She'd point out cracks in the concrete, loose parts I shouldn't step on. She would tell me I was doing fine, just a little farther to go. And pretty soon I'd be safe inside our fort, with her.

Before I started to climb the steps, I called out to her one more time.

"Natalie! Natalie where are you?"

I waited, but she didn't answer. I only heard the leaves tinkling in the breeze and the rush of wings as a solitary bluejay took flight. So I started up.

Natalie taught me this chant to say when I was climbing, so I wouldn't be afraid. "Don't look down, don't look in." I couldn't look down or I'd freeze, thinking I was going to fall. And I couldn't look in, at the dirt exposed between the slabs, because sometimes there were snakes, spiders, all kinds of things living and moving in the side of the hill. So I'd grip the concrete, half-close my eyes and feel my way up. *Don't look down, don't look in.* Natalie would guide me from above, telling me where to step, where to grab on.

But this time Natalie wasn't there.

Our fort was five steps up and just past the second vertical slab. When I got high enough, I stopped to take a breath, happy the worst part of the climb was over. I was lying flat against the concrete. The stone felt cold against my cheek and my arms hurt from the effort of holding on too tight. I started inching across the terrace step, feeling my way through the thin soles of my sandals. In places the concrete was disintegrating. Loose chunks of it would fall off if you stepped on it too hard. So I slid along the step, chanting under my breath, until I got to the vertical column. *Don't look down, don't look in.*

To cross the verticals, I had to reach over about two feet and

2

put my foot on the other side. It was easy to miss; I'd seen a boy fall and break his arm trying. So I sucked in a deep breath, reached out and found the other side. Gaining confidence, I stuck my foot out. I had just touched the concrete step across the vertical when an icy hand shot out and grabbed my ankle.

I screamed.

She giggled.

Natalie.

Here I was hugging the concrete, tears blurring my eyes, my arms scraped from the climb, and she was laughing. I was furious. And relieved. All I wanted to do was cry. But I couldn't. Natalie never cried, and she couldn't stand to see anyone else cry. I swallowed my tears as she helped me across the vertical and into our fort.

"Don't be mad Emma, I could see you the whole time. You were really good, you didn't slip once."

I smiled in spite of myself.

"I'm not mad."

I couldn't be mad at Natalie. She meant too much to me.

I grabbed a small, grungy pillow from the corner and shook it out over the edge of the terrace. Fine particles of dust caught the air and floated away. Positioning the pillow behind my head, I leaned against the wall. I could feel my heart rate slowing, the tension draining from my arms.

Our fort felt like home to me. Even though it was only another crevice between the terrace steps, it was deeper than most and showed no signs of animal life. We'd lugged up a blanket and the pillow along with some favorite objects, and we called it our secret hiding place. I loved being there, even if I hated getting there. The fort looked out between a gap in the dense line of trees to the field and the subdivision on the other side. Natalie and I would sit, nestled safely between the steps, and watch kids playing ball in the field, sweaty, bare-chested men polishing shiny cars, women in white watering bright flowering plants. From our concealed vantage point, they looked so happy.

Beside me, Natalie sprawled on her stomach, dangling a hand over the step. She rested a cheek in the crook of her elbow, her face turned away from me, her white-blond hair splayed over the red wool of the blanket.

"I want us to have a canopy bed in our house, Emma. Like my baby-sitter Tina has. Pink and frilly with big fat bows to hold it up...." Her voice sounded far away, dreamy, yet confident. Maybe that's why she seemed so grown up to me. I really believed one day we'd get married and live in a house with a canopy bed and a swimming pool.

She lapsed into silence, the twig in her hand rasping back and forth over the concrete. I watched the back of her head, waiting. I hadn't seen her all afternoon, which meant something was bothering her. Natalie always disappeared when she needed to think. Eventually I learned to let her be when she got that way. With Natalie you couldn't just ask what was wrong, you had to wait for her to tell you. So I sat quietly, dangling my legs over the terrace, my back resting against the cool clay, and watched the sky turn from blue to pink to lavender.

Natalie sat up a few minutes later. Taking my hand in hers, she brushed tenderly at the bits of concrete and pebbles still embedded in my palm. Then she laced her fingers through mine and leaned back against the wall beside me. Her arm pressed warmly against mine.

"I have to go to my dad's this weekend." She didn't look at me.

"Oh."

"So we can go skating when I get back, okay?"

"Sure." I squeezed her fingers lightly. I missed her already.

She was staring into the distance. Sunlight filtered through her golden hair and bounced off her face. She sighed and closed her eyes. How long her transparent blond eyelashes looked to me. I wanted to reach out and touch them. I thought they'd feel like feathers on my skin. She tilted her head to look at me. She didn't seem surprised to find me staring at her. Maybe she was

4

used to it.

"Can we do it again?" she whispered.

"Do what?"

I knew what she was talking about, but I felt so peaceful sitting there, and she was so beautiful just to look at. Her eyes kindled, like huge blue marbles shot with light. She sat forward and turned to face me.

"You know...only, longer this time."

I'll always remember her that way: her back to the setting sun, visible rays of light weaving paths through her fine hair; her eyes confident, yet questioning.

I didn't answer her right away. I leaned forward a little and braced a hand against the cold ground behind me. Then I raised my other hand and tentatively touched her cheek. It was warm from the sun, and soft as powder.

She smiled. Then, moving closer, she kissed me.

Chapter 2

"Shit! There's a snake in here!"

"Is it poisonous?" I asked.

"I think so. It has red rings around it's tail. Damn!"

"What level are you on?"

"Five! What should I do?" She sounded frantic.

"Did you try throwing a rock at it?"

"That just pissed it off." She let out a short scream. "It's getting closer! Come help me!"

I plucked a dish towel off the counter and walked through the living room into the den. She was sitting bolt upright, her frizzy, reddish-brown hair tucked carelessly behind her ears. I watched for a few seconds from the doorway as she pounded the keyboard trying to escape the viper. Every time she hit a key she tapped her right foot on the floor.

"Emma! Fuck, what do I do?"

"I don't know, you're the computer expert. Try blasting it with your Death Ray."

I stepped across a leaning pile of dog-eared print-outs and dodged a couple of computer manuals lying open on the floor. On the screen, a glowing S-curve advanced steadily on her valiant knight. As Carly madly punched keys, the knight hopped back and forth, hacking the air with a neon blue saber. Suddenly the viper struck. The knight wavered, then toppled to the ground, its eyes turning into little white crosses. A twangy, digital version of "Taps" issued from somewhere in back of the computer.

"Guess you're dead. Dinner's almost ready."

Carly shut off the computer, yanked the diskette from the floppy drive, and followed me out of the den, running a hand through her wild hair. She dropped the diskette on the dining room table and inhaled deeply as we entered the kitchen. The pungent aromas of garlic bread and spaghetti sauce swirled in the air, and steam rose in thick spirals from the open pots on the stove. As the pasta threatened to bubble over the edge of its huge aluminum kettle, I grabbed a wooden spoon and rushed to stir down the foam.

"Emma, where'd you get that game? It's full of bugs." Carly leaned over the sauce, a skeptical look on her face.

"From Kay. She said Marty copied a bunch of new stuff at work. That was the best one." Satisfied the pasta was now under control, I moved to the refrigerator and pulled out a head of lettuce and some tomatoes for a salad.

"I should have known. Another Kay-Mart 'Blue Light Special.' It better not infect my computer with some virus. How much garlic did you put in here?" She didn't wait for my answer, but started mincing two more cloves on the cutting board.

"I'm sure it's clean. Besides, it's free. Quit complaining. You want spring onions or bermuda in the salad?"

A close, wet heat hung in the air of the tiny kitchen. Early summer sunlight drizzled in through the greenhouse window, and steam condensed on the glass. Carly dumped the garlic into the sauce, ran her fingers through her hair again and walked out into the living room. I smiled to myself, thinking she would smell of garlic for days. Running my wrists under the cool tap, I rinsed lettuce leaves and tore them into pieces over a large glass bowl.

I felt peaceful there in Carly's home. It reminded me of my grandfather's house—the walls yellowed with age, sticky from years of cooking. Paint layered on the window sill, cracked in the corners revealing pale wood. Shadows from the branches of an old oak tree in Carly's front yard swayed across the foggy window panes.

I put the salad on the table and went to drain the pasta. Carly was now prostrate on the couch in a rare moment of relaxation, half-watching the black and white television sitting on two milk crates across the room and half-reading the newspaper that lay open on the floor in front of her. She mindlessly scratched her cat, Ruby, behind the ears.

I should make it clear that, for Carly Velasquez, doing just three things at once *is* relaxation. She hasn't stopped moving since I met her two years ago at a fund-raiser for the Gay Community Center. She was actually a friend of my former lover, Judy, but we hit it off the minute we met. As we sorted through boxes of second-hand clothing and disintegrating record albums, we discovered we both loved the theater, sappy movies and women's literature. And, since I'm being honest, women's not-so-literature, the occasional Big Mac and a certain prime-time soap opera.

She'd become my best friend even before Judy left, nursing me through the 1988 presidential election with her cutting imitation of George Bush and then through Judy's departure with her irrepressible energy. Carly simply kept me so busy I didn't have time to feel sorry for myself. Well, not much anyway. I love her with all my heart, but we've never been lovers. She's one of those people you hold so close you're past touching.

Tonight was another of our regular dinners together. Carly and I usually eat dinner together once or twice a week, although she seldom lets me cook. Carly's a whiz in the kitchen, often creating marvelous dishes from ingredients I wouldn't recognize as edible. Tonight I was on probation after a miserable attempt at Chicken Dijon that set off my fire alarm and destroyed a perfectly good casserole dish. I could tell she was keeping an eye on me even as she scanned the classifieds.

I cut the tomatoes into mushy quarters and buried them in the salad, arranging rings of red onion in a decorative pattern around the top. At least it would look good.

"Need any help, Em? I have a fire extinguisher in the closet."
She was smiling wickedly.

I stuck my tongue out, opening the oven and trying to remember what time I'd put the garlic bread in to heat.

Carly reappeared at the stove, stirring the sauce and wriggling her nostrils. I spanked her hand as she reached for the garlic again.

"Enough! We're supposed to eat this, not ward off vampires with it. Here, cut the bread."

Carly laughed and pulled a knife from the dishwasher. "You never finished your story about Kate."

"Oh, God." I rolled my eyes. "The Job From Hell, Chapter forty-two. I keep telling her to quit, but she just keeps complaining. Today she calls me up, and I can hardly hear her because she's whispering. Apparently Good Friend Harriman has taken to leaving his office door open to spy on her. So she tells me this long, drawn out story about how he made her type some memo seventeen times and then ripped it up in front of everyone in the office because she misspelled 'forensics.'"

"Forensics? What was the memo about?"

"Oh, I don't know. Some article he commissioned about that coroner in Hollywood who dissects the Stars. Anyway, she told me he called her into his office, sat her down and gave her a fifteen-minute lecture on the importance of accurate grammar."

"What an asshole." Carly plucked an onion ring off the salad and nibbled at it."I'll never forget that time she caught him going through her purse."

"Oh, I know. I caught him going through my desk one time when I worked down there. Claimed he was looking for a pen. Only there were two sticking out of his shirt pocket."

"It's great you and Kate are still so close even though you were promoted."

"Yeah. She isn't the type to envy anyone. She's so funny. She sends me these hilarious notes through inter-office mail. Today it was a picture of a hamster that said, 'Is it live or is it Hairlessman's toupee?'"

Carly laughed. "So how's your new job going, anyway?"

"Really good. I'm getting used to telling people what to do. And it's great working in the Women's Division. Remind me to show you the first proofs for this month's issue of *Perspective*. I've got them in my bag. There's a fantastic article about the Women's Festival in Antioch."

Carly grated cheese over a small bowl, and I pulled two plates from the cupboard over her head. Her hair tickled my arm.

"How's it going for you?" I glanced nervously at the classifieds, now buried beneath Ruby's voluminous fur.

Carly shrugged, banging the flat metal grater on the side of the sink. She pinched some cheese between two fingers and licked them clean.

"I don't know. Ever since they promoted that jackass Bernie, it's been hard for me to keep a positive outlook. I'm just sick of the politics, you know? Everyone's got something on everyone else. The only reason Bernie's a project manager now is because he found out Adelson is having an affair with the personnel manager."

"What?!!"

"I'm serious. Janet told me Bernie saw them coming out of some restaurant one night and casually mentioned it to Adelson the next day. Two weeks later, poof!" She snapped her fingers, "Bernie's moving his stuff into an office."

"That's unbelievable!"

I turned the pasta into a casserole dish and started to pour the sauce over it, splattering the walls and counter with little red polka dots.

"No shit. I don't know...I like what I'm doing, but I don't think I can take the bullshit anymore." She wiped part of the counter with a paper towel, her eyes glazed over in thought.

I sprinkled mozzarella over the pasta, feeling suddenly afraid. Carly rarely sounds off about anything for long without making a decision, and this one scared me. I'd known for a long time Carly wasn't happy with her job, but ever since Judy left for Oregon to pursue her career in wildlife management, I'd been crossing my fingers Carly would work it out. The thought of losing her, too, to some 'great job opportunity' hundreds of miles away filled me with dread.

She let out a sigh and smiled, wadding the paper towel into a ball and tossing it toward the trash can. She missed, but she didn't move to pick it up.

"Whatever. You gonna put that in the oven, or should I just douse it with gasoline and light a match?"

I made a face and put the casserole on the upper-most rack setting the temperature just high enough, I hoped, to melt the cheese. Carly slipped past me into the living room and turned up the TV, flopping on the couch beside Ruby and burying her hands in her hair. I watched, but she didn't look at the want ads again.

I had finished setting the table and was trying in vain to find a bottle of salad dressing with more than a few meager drops left in it, when she called to me.

"Hey, Em, didn't you used to live in Oakbrook?"

I walked out into the living room to see Carly was now sitting forward on the couch. She stared intently at the TV set.

"Yeah...why?"

"Watch."

I turned to the flickering image on the television screen. The anchorwoman had a grave expression on her face. Behind her left shoulder a graphic showed the chalk outline of a body with the words "REMAINS FOUND" in capital letters across the bottom. I sat down next to Carly, confused and a little nervous, as the scene shifted to a reporter holding a microphone. He was standing in front of a line of eucalyptus trees.

"Residents of the Oakbrook condominium complex here in North Arlington were shocked today by the grisly discovery of human remains in their own back yard. Workers demolishing the concrete earthbreak to my right reported the find to local police at about 10:00 this morning. Police chief Garrett Carter told reporters the remains appeared to be at least fifteen years old. But what stunned this quiet community was the coroner's initial report that the remains are those of a child."

A picture of Natalie's beaming face filled the small screen—her school picture, the same one that had been distributed all over the neighborhood when she disappeared. The same one she'd given to me with the words "I love you" written on the back.

"Long-time residents of this area will remember the mysterious disappearance seventeen years ago of Natalie Campbell, the eight-year-old daughter of prominent local attorney Robert Campbell. Natalie was reported missing on November 14th, 1973. Police then suspected kidnapping, but the case was never solved and Natalie's remains were never found."

The camera panned a group of men, some in uniform, others in suits and ties. They were milling around, picking their way through the rubble of broken concrete and overturned earth. Behind the cyclone fence at the top of the terrace, a crowd of mostly women and children gawked and pointed.

The demolition of the terrace had only begun. Beyond the gesturing officials, much of the concrete structure was still intact. The camera found the reporter again as he consulted a small stack of note cards.

"Pending the coroner's official investigation, police won't confirm the remains found today are those of Natalie Campbell. But if they are, investigators may finally have the clues they need to solve this seventeen-year-old mystery."

Carly turned down the volume on the set and knelt in front of me. "You okay?"

I nodded, unable to speak. I didn't know what to feel after all these years.

"That was your friend Natalie, wasn't it? You told me about her. It's incredible they didn't find her body until now."

Carly rose, giving my knee a squeeze, and went into the kitchen to finish getting dinner ready. I took the opportunity to suck in a few long, deep breaths. I concentrated on calming down, suppressing a rising tide of nausea and pushing back the nameless fear that gnawed at my stomach. The last thing I wanted to do was eat, but I got up and headed for the table anyway.

Carly brought out the garlic bread and a bowl of freshly-grated Parmesan cheese and pulled out a chair. I avoided her eyes, taking a seat across from her and hoping the low light from the chandelier and the dried flowers in the center of the small table would hide my face. My cheeks felt hot. My mouth was dry, and my hands were beginning to shake. I could feel cold shivers running up and down my arms, and I had to will myself to breathe normally. I could feel Carly looking at me as she dished pasta and salad onto her plate. She handed me a plate of spaghetti and I managed a weak smile as our eyes met.

"You want to talk about it?" She sounded doubtful, or maybe it was just my imagination. I never knew when Carly really wanted to talk and when she was just looking for me to assure her nothing was wrong.

"It's just a shock. I guess I always knew she was dead.... But I suppose you never stop hoping."

A thousand things were going through my mind, and yet I also felt completely empty. And tired, like I'd just come up from under water, from fighting a strong current, and now all I wanted was to sleep.

"Well, at least the waiting's over. You have to let yourself move on. There's nothing you can do now," Carly set the garlic bread to one side and rubbed her hands together. So simple. Just let go.

If only I could.

I dipped a fork into the pasta and curled spaghetti around the tines, my appetite gone.

"Hey, it isn't that bad, really. Or did you accidentally use Draino instead of cheese?" She was trying to cheer me up.

I gave in. "I'm sorry. It's just...I know this is going to sound weird, but I can't remember her. I've been trying to picture her in my mind, you know? But I can't. I just keep seeing that photograph."

"Well it was a long time ago. You were only—what?—eight when she disappeared."

"I know, but she was my best friend. We spent every minute together. And I can't even remember one thing we did together."

"When was the last time you thought about her?" Carly sounded sympathetic, but I knew she was making a point.

"I don't know. I can't even remember that. I feel so...guilty. Like I just gave up on her."

"Emma, she's been gone for seventeen years! Nobody expects you to carry a torch forever."

She didn't know how close she'd come to the truth.

I reluctantly lifted a fork full of pasta to my lips, too preoccupied to notice how it tasted. Natalie was dead. I knew that. I'd always known that. But somewhere in my mind I'd convinced myself she had just wandered off to think for awhile. A part of me had held on to the hope that one day I'd turn a corner and she'd jump out at me, her eyes bright, laughing and begging me not to be mad.

Carly changed the subject.

"I heard about a great job. I think I'm going to go for it. It's in San Francisco. Small company but they're doing some really interesting things. I'd go in as a Project Supervisor working on this fantastic artificial intelligence thing...."

My fork clattered to the floor. A cold metal vice slowly locked around my ribs. The buzzing in my ears grew louder and white spots danced in a whirling, liquid frenzy in front of my eyes. I struggled to stay upright, but the world was spinning around me. If I just closed my eyes, I'd be caught up in the swirling pool of white noise and whiter light....

Chapter 3

I woke up early Saturday morning. I couldn't remember coming home or going to bed. I couldn't remember anything except seeing Natalie's face, so alive, smiling out at me over the television. I lay on my back, numb, only vaguely aware of the bands of pale morning light reaching through partly closed blinds to hold up my ceiling.

I couldn't get her picture out of my mind. It blocked everything else I wanted to remember. It spread across the patterned ceiling and down the walls, crawling over my bed and enveloping me. I closed my eyes but Natalie's face filled my head, suffocating me. My eyes flew open and I gulped air, screaming silently, my fingers gripping the sheets.

Agonizing questions paralyzed me. When did I give up on Natalie? How had I lived through seventeen years without her, and *happily*? When had I gotten so old?

A rash of memories that didn't include Natalie flashed white-hot through my mind. At the beach with my mother and my grandfather, throwing soft chunks of bread into the air to be snatched up by greedy gulls. Laughing. Ice skating on the Mall, past hundreds of glowing, rosy faces in a dizzying circular parade. The cold air biting into my face. Accepting my scholarship, sweet-smelling roses cradled in my arms, the principal's rough whiskers against my cheek.

Where was Natalie? Where was she when I went to my first rock concert? Had my first date? Graduated from high school and college? Where was she when I found Judy? When I lost Judy? Why hadn't I felt the aching, hollow pain that now turned my muscles to lead and closed tight around my throat? How had I managed to ignore Natalie's relentless, consuming absence? *Why hadn't I missed her?*

Gradually, the persistent drumming in my ears resolved itself into the sounds of morning traffic outside my window. The bands of light that barely prevented the ceiling from falling in and crushing me came slowly into focus. Every square inch of my skull fought to contain an unidentified, unbearable pressure. My stomach knotted, and I tensed as another wave of fear pulsated through me. Finally, I forced myself to get up, to move.

Standing in the bathroom, running hot water in the tub, I remembered pieces of the previous night. When I got home from Carly's, Mom had left a concerned message on my answering machine. Yes, that was it, she'd invited me to come down for lunch. Said we hadn't seen enough of each other. I had a goal, a purpose. I clung to it desperately, holding on for dear life and clawing at anything else that tried to enter my mind. Anything that threatened to bring back Natalie's haunting face.

I ducked beneath the showerhead. The stinging needles pounded my back and shoulders. I let myself feel only the water racing down my arms and thighs. Dripping from my breasts and fingers. Swirling around my feet.

Washing away the pain.

After fifteen minutes, I got out of the shower, towelled off and stood before the sink, finally awake. I avoided looking in the mirror as long as I could. I knew my eyes would be puffy. Instead, when I finally faced my reflection, I looked just as I had the day before. And the day before that.

That's when I knew I hadn't cried for her.

More by instinct than by conscious decision, I followed my regular morning routine: brushing my teeth and my hair, dressing and packing my battered canvas bag with the few things I'd need for the day. At 9:30, I flipped on the answering machine, turned out the lights and opened the door to my apartment to leave.

Out in the hallway, the paper lay face up, folded in half. Just like yesterday. And the day before that. Except today a grainy reproduction of Natalie's image filled the right-hand column on the front page. The headline read *Coroner ID's remains found at Arlington condo complex.* In one angry motion, I hurled the paper through the door, and hurriedly rotated my key in the lock. I wouldn't read the story today.

Not yet.

Sitting in my filthy Celica, hands on the wheel, I made a decision. I wasn't ready to mourn Natalie, so I wouldn't try. I'd push forward, keep busy, and when I was ready, when the time was right, then I'd cry. Then I'd say good-bye. For now, I'd take it one day at a time. I had a few days of leave accrued at work, I'd take them this week and whatever happened, I'd survive. Or I wouldn't. I didn't particularly care. I just didn't want to feel the pain anymore.

I exhaled audibly, feeling the tension flow out of my neck and shoulders, and started my car.

* * * * *

It's a straight shot to my mother's house, ten miles on the expressway and a short stretch down a tree-lined parkway. So close and yet so far—we don't see each other much. But I needed her now.

I took a moment to study the little A-frame my mother calls home. She's lived alone since I left for college, my father having opted out of family life when I was three. Buying this place was her greatest achievement. It sits on nearly a fifth of an acre, no fence, and she has it painted every two years like clockwork. Today it glistened in the morning sun, recently turned a shiny pale yellow with bright white shutters framing the polished windows. I like the house. At night, the sheer curtains in the living room turn the lamplight a soft gold that beckons through the darkness. It looks like the kind of place you'd run to if you thought you were being followed. I guess it is.

I made a mental note of the additions to her flower beds knowing she'd ask, and walked inside. The screen door swung noiselessly outward at my tug, which worried me because the front door was standing wide open. I let the screen fall shut and threw its meager lock into place. "Mom?"

I passed through the spotless living room, cool despite the rising temperature outside. Mom rarely goes into the living room, preferring to spend her time in the large kitchen at the back of the house, but I think it's the most comfortable, welcoming room in the house. The sofa and armchair are upholstered in warm beige, with forest green and wine-colored throw pillows placed neatly in the corners. Cherry wood tables, dusted daily, show off framed photographs and collectibles, gifts from her many travelled friends. The room wasn't designed so much as it was lovingly brought together. And my mother fits in it perfectly.

Mom was in the kitchen, as usual, standing at the sink with her back to me, surrounded by a pile of copper pots and molds, the odds and ends which normally adorn the papered walls. She waved a plastic-gloved hand in the general direction of the dinette and kept on polishing the copper. She was on the phone—not talking, but periodically humming sympathetic agreement. I sat by the bay window, and tried to enjoy the view of Mom's backyard garden. My mother's talents are many, and she can make things grow unlike anyone I've ever known.

Finally Mom hung up the phone. "That woman couldn't reason her way out of a broom closet." She pulled off her cleaning gloves finger by finger.

"That was Felicia Thomas, who runs the literacy program. We're trying to organize a fund-raiser and all she has to do is rent the hall. So she calls and tells me she's been positively everywhere and *nothing* will do. The Hyatt's too expensive, the church is booked, the community center's roof leaks.... For God's sake, the fund-raiser's in August! What does she think, we're going to have a monsoon?"

She poured two mugs of coffee from the thermos she keeps perpetually filled and came around the counter to sit beside me. She was wearing her weekend uniform, white cotton slacks and a blue pin-striped work shirt, one of many she rescued from my grandfather's estate. "How are you, sweetheart?"

A rhetorical question. I didn't bother to answer.

She went on. "I tell you, this whole thing has me so upset...I've gotten more calls—even that witch Gladys had the nerve to phone me. You remember her, the one who lived behind the Campbells at Oakbrook? Never bathed? Well, she's smelling up some retirement community now, but apparently she still sees the news. Called me at a quarter after seven this morning to say she suspected her late husband Walter killed poor Natalie. He always hated children. Even drove her beloved son Louis to join the army and get himself killed in Vietnam. I must have been on the phone an hour with her. Remind me never to put my phone number on Christmas cards." I had to laugh. Another of my mother's talents is her ability to dramatize a conversation. She can imitate anyone. She's nearly fifty, but still slim and energetic. Through the miracle of modern technology, her hair is a variegated blonde, cut short and styled to sweep up at the back. Her eyes are a threatening hazel when they want to be, and her nose and mouth move in unison when she talks. She actually looks a lot like Candice Bergen. It's eerie.

She uncrossed her legs and reached over to hold my hand. "So? How are you? Talk to me."

I squeezed her fingers affectionately. "I'm okay, I guess. I don't know what to think. I suppose there'll be some huge investigation.... It's the news reports I can't take. Seeing her picture. She looks so young. I guess in my mind she aged with me. It just reminds me of how long its been." I took a long drink of coffee, thankful for the warmth spreading down my throat.

Mom got up again and picked up a dishrag. She wiped off the counter, although I had spilled nothing on it.

"Well, honey, it was just a matter of time. When they didn't find her those first few weeks, I knew she wasn't coming back. It's just a shame, she was such a beautiful girl. That blond hair...and you two were so close."

A blinding ribbon of pain shot through my chest, punching the air out of my lungs. Memories, frozen in time like snapshots, flashed behind my closed eyelids. Kissing Natalie, our eyes open, our mouths firmly, innocently, closed; holding her butter-soft hand; watching her run ahead of me on long, athletic legs and then stop and turn to urge me on. I sucked down some more coffee, burning my tongue. I found myself confessing, "I loved her."

I'd never said those words to her.

Mom kept tidying. "Well of course you did. You were like sisters, we couldn't pry you two apart." She started busily drying a copper mold that was shaped like a rooster.

"No, Mom. I mean I *really* loved her."

I met her eyes, begging her to understand. She'd known I was a lesbian for four years now, but she had never quite believed love between women could be as passionate, as consuming, as the heterosexual love she knew.

Her hands still rubbed the shiny orange metal, the yellow cloth moving in small concentric circles. She looked at me, frowning slightly, trying to read me. Trying to figure out what to say.

"This is about being a lesbian. You think Natalie was a lesbian, too? She was only eight years old...."

"No, Mom, that's not what I'm saying." My hands tightened around the coffee mug in frustration. "I don't know if Natalie was a lesbian. I just know how I felt. I loved her. I wanted to be with her. In some ways, I consider her to be my first lover."

"Oh, for God's Sake, Emma. That's ridiculous. You were just children." She turned away and started running water in the sink.

Normally I would have given up at this point. Let Mom consider what I'd said in her own time. But this was different. I got up and went into the kitchen to stand beside her.

"Mom, I know this is hard for you to understand. It's hard for me to explain. What I mean is, I felt...connected to Natalie. The same way I feel now about a lover. I've never felt that way about a man."

She peered at me, uncomprehending. "But you went with that Eric for so long. Didn't you feel something?"

We'd had this conversation before. I knew she was trying to understand. She'd accepted my lesbianism, but she'd never really understood it. She'd never believed I could be truly happy without loving a man. Without being married and having children. She worried about the struggle I faced being gay, being "so different." Sometimes she'd ask me about gay-related controversies she'd seen in the news, like the Mapplethorpe exhibit, efforts to pass a national hate crimes bill, the AIDS epidemic. I'd tell her what I knew. Sometimes I'd give her articles and pamphlets I thought might help, but my world still seemed separate from her. She worried about me getting lost and hurt in a place where she couldn't protect me.

"I did feel something for Eric, but not like I felt for Judy. He never really listened to me or understood me. We could be sitting in the same room and I'd feel completely alone. With Judy, the connection was elemental. I could talk to her about anything, and I could tell what she was feeling. It was that way with Natalie, too, but of course we were so young, I didn't realize it at the time."

Mom rinsed a glass under the running water, picking at some unseen spot with a long fingernail. I waited, tense, feeling little drops of water bounce off the glass and hit my hand where it rested on the sink.

"Do you ever hear from Judy?" She reached for the handle to the dishwasher and I stepped aside to let her open the door.

I relaxed a little. I knew Mom had heard all she was capable of hearing for awhile. Educating her about my emotional life was an incremental process. Each time we talked about it, she came a little closer to realizing what it meant for me to love women. But she couldn't take it in all at once.

"She writes occasionally. She's still in Oregon counting endangered marshland species. I guess she's happy. Spends most of her time outdoors. That's what she wanted."

Mom dried her hands and replaced the dishrag over the oven door, carefully folding it into thirds and centering it on the steel bar. She passed by me and patted my arm.

"I still miss her." When Judy had left to pursue her career, Mom had treated it at first like any good friend moving away. Gradually she had come to realize the pain ran far deeper than that. That the loss compared more closely to the day my father packed his bags and took off.

"I called the Campbells this morning." Mom took her seat at the dinette again and reclaimed her coffee mug. "Robert seemed shaken but he's handling it well. He's not the type to let strong emotion show."

"What did he say? How's Angela?"

"I gather she's not taking it very well. Robert said she was lying down when I called. She was so strong when Natalie disappeared, I guess she's been holding it in a long time."

"It must be awful for her. To have the police questioning her and reporters all over her, especially now. I wonder how she feels having Natalie called Robert's daughter in all the press reports? I mean they hardly even mention her."

Mom nodded. "He did adopt Natalie not long after they were married. He's well-known down here. They say he may enter politics next year. Lieutenant governor or some such. I see his picture in the paper all the time, shaking hands with senators, accepting humanitarian awards."

"I've always thought a Republican humanitarian award was an oxymoron."

Mom laughed. She's less political than I am, but she appreciates the editorial cartoons I send her. I'm trying to get her to consistently vote the Democratic ticket, but she still thinks "liberal" equals "higher taxes." She drank some more coffee.

"In those publicity shots, Angela's always standing right behind Robert. I saw them in the paper just a few weeks ago. She looks so elegant. I remember when she wore her hair in those awful clips, no make-up. Now she's wearing diamonds and designer gowns. It's funny."

"What do you mean?"

"Oh, just the irony of it. She's lived a Cinderella life ever since she married Robert: beautiful houses, jewelry, clothes. Now this. Your grandfather always used to say the higher you fly, the harder you fall...."

"Yeah, but he also had that Robert Frost poem, 'The Road Not Taken,' framed in his den."

"I don't suppose marrying well can be considered taking the least-travelled road." Mom's expression changed with the mention of my grandfather.

I took her hand. "He'd be proud of you, Mom. You didn't settle for the easy way out."

She looked at me, her fingers closing around mine.

"He'd be proud of you, too, sweetheart. I know I am."

Mom disengaged her fingers from mine and collected our mugs, returning to the kitchen once again. I glanced at the wall above the table, at the framed picture of my grandfather that my mother had moved from the living room into this room. It looked out of place in the kitchen, a powerful portrait of him standing tall in a three-piece suit, his hands clasping the cane he refused to use, but she wanted to have it where she'd see it every day. I stared into his impenetrable gray eyes, wondering what he would have said to me today. How he would have put Natalie's death into perspective, made it mean something. Then I smiled, thinking he would have let me figure it out for myself. I missed him.

"He asked about you."

I jumped, looking from the picture to my mother and back again. "Who?"

"Robert. He asked about you."

I blushed, chiding myself for actually thinking...what *was* I thinking?

"Robert's always one for remembering names. Helps in running for office, I suppose. I get the feeling he has a little box full of index cards by the phone so when someone calls he can ask the right questions. He knew I was on the Literacy Commission, although for the life of me I can't imagine how. Even volunteered to speak if we needed him to. Gave me the name of this Personal Private Executive Secretary. Wilson somebody-or-other. I think he answered the phone when I called. 'Campbell residence, may I inquire who's calling? Very good, madam.'" Mom assumed a British accent, miming a hand twisting the end of a handlebar mustache.

"He did not say that!"

"Well, something like that. Robert said they've planned a memorial service for Monday morning, but they're 'receiving visitors' this afternoon if you want to drop by."

My heart landed in my stomach at the thought of facing Robert and Angela after all these years.

"From 2 to 4:30 sharp. I wish I could go, but I have to help that nitwit Felicia find a hall for the fund-raiser. You have to tell me what their house looks like. I've heard it's spectacular."

She already knew I was going to see the Campbells. "Can I borrow a dress? I don't think they'd appreciate army surplus."

Chapter 4

As Angela puttered about the kitchen, Natalie and I knelt at the coffee table piecing together a puzzle. It was almost finished, a gauzy picture of a three-story Victorian doll house. The living room in the miniature house contained a glittering Christmas tree covered with tiny white lights. In the bedroom, a mommie doll tucked her doll children into a lacy, overstuffed bed. On the roof, Santa was just preparing to slide down the chimney.

Natalie's house was warm, despite the bitter December wind outside. Sammy Davis, Jr., played on the turntable, and Natalie and I were racing to be the one to put the last puzzle piece in place.

Angela came out of the kitchen wearing a red gingham apron and stirring the contents of a beige ceramic bowl with a long wooden spoon. She paused behind Natalie, smiling down at us. Her nose and chin were dusted with flour, and her shoulder-length hair was pulled back from her face with two tortoise-shell combs.

She held the handle of the spoon to her lips to signal me into silence. Then, setting the bowl soundlessly on the floor beside her, she positioned herself on her knees behind Natalie. She watched us, holding her breath, until only two loose puzzle pieces remained.

I picked up one of the pieces and slipped it into place, watching a beaming smile of victory spread across Natalie's face. She reached across the table for the last piece just as Angela caught her in her arms. Quickly, I dropped the last piece into the puzzle and fell over laughing. Natalie squirmed in her mother's arms, turning to blow a wet raspberry kiss against Angela's neck.

Angela rescued the ceramic bowl and scooped a big mound of chocolate chip cookie dough onto the wooden spoon. She broke off large, sticky pieces for Natalie and me and sat licking her fingers while we ate.

"Natalie, do you like my friend Robert?" Angela kept stirring the dough and not looking at us, but I could tell Natalie's answer was important to her.

Natalie reached for the wooden spoon and held it between us so we could both eat off it. "I guess so."

"What do you like about him?"

"He's nicer than Daddy. He doesn't throw things. And I like the radio and the doll he gave me."

We were silent for a few seconds, Angela watching Natalie intently with a thoughtful smile on her face. She brushed a stray lock of hair from Natalie's cheek.

"Is Robert going to be my new Daddy?"

Angela didn't answer, but straightened out her apron, and replaced a loose comb in her hair.

"Would you like that?"

"I guess."

She smiled down at Natalie, whose lips were now covered with melted chocolate and bits of cookie dough. Retrieving the bowl and spoon Angela returned to the kitchen, humming "The Candyman."

Chapter 5

I felt ambivalent about seeing the Campbells again. A part of me wanted to be with them, to share in their grief. To find out how to grieve. But the address at the bottom of my mother's carefully written directions kept reminding me they weren't the same people, the second family, I remembered.

Robert and Angela Campbell had married when Natalie and I were four. He moved into Angela's townhouse at Oakbrook, but once his legal career took off they didn't stay long. Since Natalie's disappearance, they'd lived in five different homes, each larger and more luxurious than the last. Their latest address was off Blue Falls Drive, about as upwardly mobile as you can get without leaving Northern Virginia.

With my weathered map spread out on the passenger seat, I navigated the parkway and pushed the Celica up several tributary roads until I reached Blue Falls Drive, the winding, shaded road that runs the length of the low hills bordering the Potomac. Up here, the houses are set so far from the street you can't see them at all. But once inside, they afford a priceless view of the river and the spires of Washington Cathedral.

I must have driven a quarter of a mile before the trees began to thin and the road to widen. Suddenly the edifice of a massive white columned house came into view and the drive ballooned out before it. A uniformed security guard holding a clipboard stopped me and I rolled down the window. A blast of hot, wet air hit my face.

"Your name?"

"Emma Kendrick. I'm here to see the Campbell's."

He checked the clipboard and scanned the back seat, apparently satisfied with what he found. Or didn't find.

"Sorry, ma'am. Just trying to keep the press out. You can park anywhere in front of the house."

He waved me on and I rolled the window back up. I saw another man in uniform standing across the courtyard by what I assumed was the exit. No one else was in sight.

I hid the Celica off to one side under a lavish oleander—sure that, if I didn't, the car would be towed under some rarely-used aesthetics clause in the Virginia penal code. Several other vehicles parked unabashedly close to the entry, among them a BMW, a Lincoln Continental and a white stretch limousine. I decided not to bother locking the Celica. I stepped out of the car, still hidden in the shade of the sweet-smelling hedge, and brushed some imagined dust off the navy suit my mother had loaned me.

Before I could get close enough to knock, one of the double doors beneath the wide entryway opened, and a face I recognized from the news brushed past me. I couldn't pin a name on him, but I was sure he had something to do with the Governor's office or the state legislature. Two indistinguishable grey-suited men followed him, along with a small, pained-looking woman I knew must have had a face lift.

A graven-faced man in severe black reluctantly held the door open for me. He gave me the once-over as I passed through the doorway, probably scanning for suspicious bulges in my pockets. I noticed he and I were the same height. He did too.

"I am Wilson Bennett, Mr. Campbell's secretary. May I tell Mr. Campbell who is calling?" He closed the door soundlessly behind me.

"Emma Kendrick. I'm a friend of..." I wanted to claim my friendship with Natalie. But with all the years, and no tears yet, I couldn't. I added lamely, "...a friend of the family."

I followed Bennett into the front room, and obediently sat

where he indicated. He nodded solemnly and drifted back through the archway.

The living room looked like something out of Architectural Digest. Over inlaid parquet floors, someone had spread a spongy layer of snow white carpeting, the same color as the walls and furniture: a velvet sofa with two matching wing chairs. Like dead tree stumps rising through the snow, two huge black vases containing long feathery dried stems of pale wheat and deep blue flanked the marble fireplace.

A square coffee table topped with half-inch thick greenish glass lurked like a sinkhole in the center of the room and threatened to suck me in. Several mammoth paintings hung on the walls, mostly geometric designs in black lacquered frames. Other than a curving black metal lamp that reached outward like a claw from behind the couch, the only light source visible in the room was the massive paned picture window that ran the width of the room. The black and white striped drapes were open, affording a view of Washington I expected made up at least 20 percent of the property's value. I tried to sit up straight.

After nearly fifteen minutes, Robert and Angela finally entered the room. Angela took a seat on the sofa sitting so far forward she didn't even dent the cushions. She had on a black linen suit with an ivory blouse, a striking gold pin attached to the lapel. Her hair, a lighter shade of blonde than I remembered, was fashioned into a soft chignon and she wore heavy gold earrings. Her smile didn't extend to her green eyes, and she nervously twisted a lace-edged handkerchief in her hands.

When she didn't speak, I turned hopefully to Robert, who stood between us looking out the window, his arms clasped behind his back. His taste in clothes had improved with his income—he was immaculate in a black pin-striped suit and striped silk tie. He wore a silver tie bar and a pearl-grey silk handkerchief folded into three points in his jacket pocket. His hair had greyed exactly the way it's supposed to, just a little at the temples and the sides. Otherwise he looked much as I remembered him: tall, broad-shouldered, handsome in a planned sort of way. His eyes and hair were the same chocolate brown, and he was tan, even behind the ears.

"Emma, it's good to see you again. Angela and I appreciate your stopping by." He spoke with the precise modulation of someone whose native language isn't English.

"I'm so sorry."

I didn't know what else to say. I've never known anyone who died except my grandfather, and then I had been on the other side of the receiving line. The stiff collar on Mom's suit dug into my neck.

"It's been quite a shock," Robert said. "And of course the media are very persistent. We decided it would be easier on our friends and family if we scheduled a time they could visit without fear of being filmed or photographed. I suppose it's to be expected, but it is such a strain on Angela."

He moved toward his wife and extended a hand to her. Anglea wrapped her fingers around his and he sat down in the wing chair next to her. "I hope you don't mind if I relax. We've had a tiring day already."

"Oh, of course not. I'm so sorry."

It occurred to me now might be a good time to dive into the black-hole coffee table. Robert massaged his temples, apparently waiting for me to continue. I said, "I thought I recognized the man leaving just now...."

Robert's brows shot up. "What man?"

"He was with two other men and an older woman. I thought I'd seen him on the news."

He seemed relieved. "That must be John Sowers. He's with the governor's office."

He waved a hand as if to erase his show of concern. "Sorry if I snapped. I thought maybe you'd seen Frank Mercer. He's been hanging around here lately. The staff have orders to notify the police if he shows up again."

So that was it. Frank Mercer was Angela's first husband and

Natalie's natural father. His alcoholism had destroyed their marriage; he was a mean drunk. As far as I knew he'd been in and out of treatment with little success ever since.

"I didn't realize he still lived in Virginia."

"Yes, oh yes. Showed up yesterday in a thirty-dollar suit and polyester tie looking around for the cameras. Claims he's on the wagon for good. I don't believe it." Robert rubbed his palms against his eyes and raked his fingers through his hair, taking care to pat it back into place.

"Now, Robert, he just wanted to express his sympathy. She was his daughter too."

Angela's voice startled me—she'd been so deathly quiet. She reached over and patted her husband's knee in a way that reminded me of a mother telling her son to sit still.

"Sympathy? He's looking for a hand-out, Angela, just like he always has. He's only out for himself. Mark my words, he's looking for a way to profit from this even now."

"Robert. Please! Emma doesn't want to hear this." Her voice had a sing-song quality that sounded forced.

Robert closed his eyes for an instant, taking a deep breath to calm himself. When his eyes opened again, they were focused on me and held none of the anger I'd seen moments ago.

"I understand you're working for a publishing firm, Emma. Associate editor, isn't that right?" Mom had been right; Robert had cross referenced me in his index cards.

"Yes, Brown & Phillips. We publish public interest magazines and newspapers. I'm responsible for a small division, mostly women's publications."

"Very commendable. I have several friends in the publishing field. I'd be happy to introduce you."

"I appreciate that. Actually I'm still learning. I just got promoted."

"Well, I'm sure you'll be very successful. Washington's a good place to be for publishing. Everyone wants to see their name in print."

A full-blown image of the headline in this morning's paper popped painfully into my mind.

"I've found that out. We get a lot of offers from the Hill to write articles. Unfortunately, members of Congress don't always take our deadlines seriously."

Robert nodded absentmindedly. I glanced over at Angela and saw she wasn't listening either. The smile was gone, her features frozen. Her eyes focused unseeing into the murky depths of the coffee table. For an instant, I was afraid she was going to jump in.

My heart went out to her, having to entertain at a time like this. I sincerely doubted if even Robert's iron will could contain his emotions much longer. I've never understood why people are forced to share their grief with others. When my grandfather died, all I had wanted was to be alone.

I felt compelled to break the silence.

"I understand you're considering a run for office. My mother mentioned you might be interested in the lieutenant governorship?"

It was a ridiculous thing to say, but Robert obviously didn't want to talk about Natalie, and my asking about the police investigation was out of the question.

"Of course that's all up in the air now. I've been approached to consider the position, but my family comes first. I'm sure I won't be making that decision for some time."

I was sorry I'd asked. I wanted to tell him it was okay to be himself, to show what he was feeling. But I knew it was a lost cause. Robert reminded me of Eric, always budgeting his emotional time. I imagined him later locking himself into a darkened den to nurse his grief alone over a bottle of 12-year-old Scotch.

We sat in silence again, Angela occasionally pressing the handkerchief to her lips. I was about to get up to leave when Bennett appeared in the archway separating the living room from the foyer.

"A call for you, sir. Senator Randolph's office."

Robert politely excused himself. I wanted to follow him out but Angela stopped me.

"Emma, it's been so long since we saw you last. You look wonderful. Do forgive me for being so preoccupied." She turned a little to lean on the arm of the sofa.

"Oh, of course. My mother mentioned that you were receiving visitors this afternoon, and I just thought I should come to tell you how sorry I am." For the third time.

She turned away and gazed, unseeing, out the window. I felt like a voyeur.

"Thank you, dear. It has been a shock. I guess I never let go of the hope she'd come back some day.... And then the days turn into weeks and the weeks to years. They always say it's better to know once and for all. Don't believe them."

She was talking more to herself than to me. She seemed disillusioned, angry. I got angry, too, thinking of what the reporters must be putting her through. I moved to the couch to offer her my hand. She smiled and took it immediately, wrapping both her hands and the handkerchief around it.

"Oh, Emma. I look at you and I can't help wondering how Natalie would have turned out. You're so beautiful and independent. Just like your mother. She must be so proud."

I smiled, thinking how different my mother was from this perfectly groomed, isolated being. And how wrong she was about me. Looking down, I saw her nail polish, a pale, pearly pink, chipping at the edges. She patted my hand and disengaged one of her own to wipe a silent tear from her cheek.

"I guess so. She wanted me to tell you she's sorry she couldn't come. She's working on a fund-raiser for the Literacy Commission."

"Oh, that's all right. Seeing you is just like seeing her anyway. You look so much alike. I remember when the four of us went places, everyone always knew whose daughter was whose."

"Natalie did look a lot like you."

"She did, didn't she...?" Angela looked out the window again, her eyes misting over.

"I'm sorry. I shouldn't have said that."

She squeezed my hand. "No, you're right. She was a lot like me. She needed me. But I couldn't protect her. There was nothing else I could do...."

Her grip on my hand tightened and she took long deep breaths, closing her eyes for a few seconds. Then she straightened up, blinked a few times and focused fully on me.

"I thank you for coming. It's been far too long. I know Bobbie will be sorry she missed you."

"How is she?"

"Oh, she's fine. She just graduated from college, George Washington University. She's going to law school, just like her father."

"That's wonderful. I can't believe she's grown up. The last time I saw her she was your new baby. Natalie's new little sister."

"Robert's pride and joy. She's quite a young lady now, and the image of her father."

"I hope I see her again."

"You must come to the memorial service, of course. It's Monday morning, ten-thirty, at St. Anthony's. And please tell your mother to come. I'd love to see her again."

"I will."

Her eyes moved past me to the doorway and I turned to see Robert conferring with Bennett in the foyer. He came into the room looking a little better than he had when he left.

"Angela, darling, the senator and his wife will be stopping by at three o'clock. Perhaps you'd like to freshen up?"

I gladly took my exit cue. Angela stood and joined her husband at a long, bevelled glass mirror so subtly placed I hadn't noticed it before. He turned away from it and Angela began to straighten his tie. I waited for them to finish, not wanting to slip out without a proper good-bye.

"When is Bobbie coming home?" Robert didn't seem to realize

I was still in the room. I glanced away, pretending to study an artist's rendition of what looked like a pair of dice on a blood-red background.

"She'll be here soon." Angela was placating him, using the same tone my mother used with the more paranoid members of her committee.

"It doesn't look right, her not being here. She should be with the family, not off telling some stranger her problems."

"She's having a difficult time, Robert. She just needs someone to talk to. I'm sure she'll be back any minute."

"Well, mother isn't going to be happy if she isn't here when she gets back."

"I'm sure she will be. Don't worry."

So far I'd counted fourteen dots on one die and eleven on the other. I began to study the signature, a straight line with three slashes through it. Xavier Xandrax?

Since they'd forgotten me, I moved on toward the door. Then it opened, flooding the foyer in bright light. I turned to see two women walking through the doorway.

"I mean it, Barbara, this is no time for you to be neglecting your father...." The older woman saw me and stopped, gripping the younger woman's arm as if in warning.

I recognized Lillian Campbell at once. She was petite and beautifully groomed, her silver hair sweeping up to emphasize her smooth forehead. She gave me an almost suspicious look, but I didn't pay much attention. My gaze was fixed on the younger woman.

What a beauty Bobbie Campbell had become. With her father's dark eyes, her short brown hair turning to flame in the harsh sunlight. She stood nearly six feet, with wide shoulders and slim hips. Her luminous eyes drew me like a magnet so that I stared openly into them. She stared back.

Lillian's voice broke the spell, "I didn't realize we had a guest." She came forward and extended her hand to me. "I'm Lillian Campbell, Robert's mother."

Her son intervened. "This is Emma Kendrick, mother. You may remember she and Natalie were very close."

"I'm so sorry, Mrs. Campbell." I mumbled my sympathies, all too aware of Bobbie moving closer to me.

"And Emma surely you remember Barbara." Lillian pulled Bobbie forward.

She spoke to me. "Hello, Emma."

I took her hand and looked back into those eyes. They were bright, almost mischievous. She released my hand slowly, brushing her fingertips hotly against mine.

Robert's voice cut through the electric air between us. "Well, Emma was just leaving. We'll see you Monday, then. And thank you again for coming."

Bennett appeared out of nowhere and opened the door for me, standing stock straight and tilting his head back to make him seem taller. I nodded and took my leave, my hand still burning from Bobbie's touch.

The door closed noiselessly behind me. Goosebumps stood on my arms. A cold shiver passed up my spine. I saw that picture of Natalie behind my eyes, her marble blue eyes beseeching me. I remembered her soft lips pressing against mine, her hot breath on my cheek. Guilt spread through my veins. *What was I doing?* I could feel Natalie falling farther away from me.

Remember! I had to remember. I brushed my hands together to rid them of Bobbie's memory. Somewhere in my mind I knew I had blamed Bobbie for taking Natalie away. Why? I walked to the car afraid to look back at the house. She was watching me, I knew it. Somehow she was going to take Natalie away again.

Chapter 6

It was nearing four o'clock when I pulled into the Oakbrook condominium complex. Few people were about, but I could hear the high-pitched laughter of children playing in the park behind the unbroken line of townhouses.

The complex had changed little in the ten years since my mother and I moved out. I could see that a few of the scrawny trees the developer had planted had taken root. In places, the branches reached out over the wall to cast mottled shadows on the asphalt. Several dented compact cars struggled to stay cool in the rare pools of shade.

The complex was divided into two distinct parts. The first was smaller and overlooked the park. The second, the one Natalie and I had lived in, consisted of five rows of identical two-story homes separated by a paved walkway that snaked around the end units and provided an excellent, if noisy, skating surface. A long pitted driveway ran down the length of the complex and curled back around the second division, forming a squared-off figure six.

I reached the second part of the complex and looked up to what had been my mother's bedroom window. White venetian blinds now hung crookedly where she had once placed blue chintz curtains. Through the open gate, the backyard seemed barren compared to the profuse greenery she had managed to cram into its meager space. Other than that, it looked much the same as it had when I was eight. When, every day after school, I

37

would come running down the drive and throw the gate open to run through the house and come out the other side, looking for Natalie.

Around the front of our unit and across the walkway, Natalie's old house also looked much the same. Someone along the line had chosen to repaint the front door blue. A questionable improvement over the sickening shade of green it had been, a legacy of the tenants two families before Natalie's. I didn't stop to study her house, but continued down the drive toward the back of the complex and the terrace.

As I walked along, memories seeped under the steel door in my mind—the mental barrier I had erected seventeen years ago. Happy images appeared—Natalie and I spying on the old man in 1408 who used to sit on his front stoop and eat yellow corn from the can. Muscular teenage boys careening down the drive in their souped-up Mustangs, tossing beer cans against the stucco walls. The time Natalie and I got hold of a box of matches and sat behind the dumpsters setting fire to everything we could find that would burn.

At last I came to the fence that marked the end of the property and ran along the top of the terrace. I slowed my pace, listening for voices, but heard only a dog barking somewhere behind me. The ancient cyclone fence was listing in places, curling up at the bottom and sagging at the top. I found a spot where the wire was peeling back enough to let me pass without destroying Mom's navy skirt. In one brave motion, I shoved myself through.

I picked my way across the sloping ground, ducking the branches of a few stunted trees, until I stood in full view of the terrace and the creek bed. An abandoned yellow backhoe rested diagonally at the bottom of the terrace, its scoop still partially filled with debris. The demolition crew had apparently just begun to excavate the terrace, starting at the top and working down the first section, then pulling out most of the rows in the second section. Near the bottom, a thick slab of the concrete lay at an uncertain angle. The lower end pointed to what I knew had been Natalie's grave.

Yellow crime-scene tape anchored by long thin stakes fluttered in the breeze, marking a shallow pit in the ground and cordoning off the area for several feet in every direction. The earth was scarred with hundreds of footprints, and as I got closer I could see finger-sized holes where a tripod had stood. Someone had stabbed a shovel into the ground below the pit. I felt for a second that if I pulled it out, the earth would bleed.

I didn't cross the ominous yellow boundary, but stood for a while taking it all in. I felt numb, distant from everything I was seeing.

I realized painfully that my few memories of this place were more real to me than it's physical form. I turned my back on the scene, retracing my steps. Just before I ducked through the fence I took one last look at the raw wound where Natalie's remains had been found. It was then I realized that she had been buried directly beneath our fort.

* * * * *

Walking slowly, I followed the winding path past house after house, noticing how each of the families who lived in the complex had tried to make the cookie-cutter homes individual in some way. Wreaths of dried flowers or pine cones hung on many of the doors, each a little different from the others. Although I knew the houses came with drapes, only a few of the windows showed tell-tale beige. I could see translucent sheers, vertical blinds in various colors, complicated treatments that depended on heavy brocade to hold the fabric back. Clusters of potted plants huddled on doorsteps, and flourishing vines cascaded from the balconies overhead. Several of the condos were vacant, iridescent "For Sale" signs creaking in the afternoon breeze.

As I approached Natalie's house, I let my thoughts turn back to why I was here. I wanted to remember her. To fix her in my mind forever, so no one could ever take her away again.

Our bedrooms had faced each other across the walkway on

the second floor. At night we'd open our windows and call across to each other, giggling so loudly we woke the neighbors. When we didn't want to say goodnight, we'd leave the windows open and go to sleep knowing we could wake each other up if we needed to.

Natalie's was often the last voice I heard at night and the first I heard in the morning. We'd make our plans for the day before we ever stepped out of bed, then get dressed and meet on the path to go play. Sometimes we'd race—I'd come out of the house panting and pushing my fist through a sleeve only to find her lying on the pebbled walkway pretending to sleep. I'd step on her lightly and she'd wake up, saying she'd been waiting for 'hours and hours'. Then she'd tag me and run wildly down the drive toward the terrace.

We'd only known each other for a few years, yet my entire childhood was wrapped in her memory, and bolted behind the door in my mind. I couldn't picture myself playing with anyone else. When she disappeared, my childhood ended. And now I'd forgotten so much of what we shared. I tried in vain to conjure images of us at school, at birthday parties, or on camping trips. We'd done so much, yet only hazy images remained. I wanted to remember everything, every moment. My head ached with the effort.

"That's where the dead girl lived, you know."

I jumped at the gravelly voice and whipped around, almost knocking over a plump elderly woman carrying a massive grey Persian cat.

"Oh! I'm so sorry, you startled me." I could feel my heart beating in my chest as I helped to steady her.

"Not to worry, not to worry. I teeter and totter, but I don't fall down." She patted one end of the cat with a gnarled hand. "Don't live here, do you? I know just about everybody lives here."

"No.... I used to. When I was a child."

"I saw you lookin' at the dead girl's house. Thought you might be with the papers...?" Her eyes, a glassy, twinkling blue that matched the highlights in her hair, were wide with anticipation.

In fact, everything about her was blue. Her dress was a floral print in varying shades of blue and purple and she had a large blue purse slung around her wrist. She wore a brilliant, square-cut blue sapphire on the third finger of her left hand, the hand that still rested on the faceless cat. Even her shoes were blue. She looked vaguely familiar.

"No, I'm not with the press. I...I used to know the girl."

"Oh, well, so did I. Lived here thirty years, I have. Seen 'em come, seen 'em go. Don't miss much of what goes on around here. Keep it all locked away, you know, just in case."

She tapped the side of her head, disturbing the cat. Its orange eyes opened in a discontented glare, then closed, disappearing again into mounds of fur.

"I see. You must have some interesting stories to tell." I said it out of habit. I had volunteered at a nursing home in high school, and whenever I couldn't think of anything to say to one of the elderly residents, that's the line I'd use. I learned more about American history sitting in that visitors' lounge than I learned in all my high school civics classes.

"Why don't you come inside and I'll fix us some tea. Tell you about the time I helped catch a vicious burglar. Stole all my silver, he did. Got it back though. Sent him up the river for ten years...."

I followed the woman, taking tiny steps to avoid treading on her heels as she led the way to a house three doors down from where I used to live. That's when I remembered who she was. Dorothy Huntemann, an institution of sorts at Oakbrook, one of the original tenants. We used to go by her house five or six times on Halloween to get her homemade brownies. Each time we knocked at her door, she'd pretend she hadn't seen us before, exclaiming with delight at our costumes and trying in vain to guess who we were. My mother loved her. She swore Mrs. Huntemann was the only person on earth who could make tulips

41

grow year-round.

Mrs. Huntemann hadn't changed much, although I guessed her to be in her mid-eighties now. She picked through a number of keys on a ring attached to a silver whistle and chose one. Inserting it in the lock, she rotated the bolt, nearly capsizing the cat in the process. It dropped to the floor inside the door and sauntered into the living room, hoisting its considerable mass into an armchair and immediately falling asleep again.

"You just sit yourself down and I'll go get the tea things. Don't mind Tinkerbell, she'll move if you tell her to." Mrs. Huntemann's bent form disappeared through a doorway and I took a seat near the window. As I passed her chair, Tinkerbell opened an eye that said loud and clear, "Don't even think about it."

With heavy burgundy drapes obscuring all but a sliver of the light from the window, I needed a moment for my eyes to adjust to the darkness in the living room. Several lamps were turned on, but their pleated silk shades allowed only a small amount of illumination to escape.

This was some living room. Aside from the armchairs Tinkerbell and I occupied, there was a pudgy green sofa that barely supported over a dozen needlepoint throw pillows. Two squat tables were jammed between the chairs and sofa, forcing me to sit at an odd angle to avoid eating my knees. More tables scattered throughout the room buckled under the weight of porcelain figurines, framed photographs, and the odds and ends of a long and remarkable lifetime. A bloated ceramic Buddha surveyed the room through slit eyes from atop a priceless rolltop desk, and on the floor beside the sofa a stack of recent magazines attested to Mrs. Huntemann's wide range of interests, from gardening to Christian Science to current events.

I was studying a sepia photograph of what I guessed to be her college graduating class when Mrs. Huntemann came back into the room loaded down with a china teapot, two cups and a plate of brownies on a silver serving tray.

"That's right, I'm a college graduate, I am. You won't find many of us my age. My father told me when I got out of high school, 'Dorothy,' he said, 'I sent six sons to college, I don't see why I shouldn't send you.' Had a marvelous time, I did. Recommend it. You go to college, did you?"

I helped her clear a space for the tea tray, and set out the two delicate china cups on saucers for her to pour. "Yes, I did. Rice University. It's in Houston."

"Oh, I know where it is. I know where just about everything is. Comes from reading all the time." She gestured to the pile of magazines and two floor-to-ceiling bookcases that bulged with well-thumbed volumes whose titles I couldn't read. "Pretty place, Texas. Don't like the heat, though. And it's too flat. A person needs to see some hills every now and then, else she forgets how to climb."

"You sound like my mother. She works with the Literacy Commission."

"Well good for her. It's a tragedy anyone in this country grows up not knowing how to read. Only way to learn anything. You give me the address and I'll send her a check. I'm always ready to spend a few dollars where I know it's goin' to help someone." She watched me bite into a brownie.

"You still like those, I see. You never could get enough of my brownies."

She surprised me. "You remember me?"

"Course I do." She grinned proudly. "Took me a bit, but then I reckoned back to when that little girl was alive and I remembered you two racing around here together. Two peas in a pod, you were."

"Yes, we were." I sipped my tea, feeling the liquid dissolve the iron knot in my chest.

Mrs. Huntemann deftly changed the subject.

"How's your momma, she still trying to grow tulips in winter?"

"No," I laughed. "She gave that up a long time ago. I think

she knew when she was beaten."

"Well, I'll tell you a secret I never told your momma." She leaned forward conspiratorially. "I bring my bulbs inside and set 'em on the stove every night. Makes 'em think its spring out. Then I put 'em outside every day, just to see the look on your momma's face."

"Oh no! She tried so hard to figure out how you did it."

"I suppose you can tell her now. She's old enough to know. Tell her it's just my way of keeping her on her toes."

We drank our tea in silence for a few minutes. It tasted like spearmint and lemon, reminding me of summers spent on the Maryland shore.

I felt peaceful sitting among the bric-a-brac of Mrs. Huntemann's life, listening to Tinkerbell snore softly in the chair next to mine. I wanted to curl up and fade into the comfort of the chair just like the cat—carefree, well-fed, knowing if I needed to feel the soft touch of another human being, someone was there. Suddenly I missed Judy with a force I hadn't felt in months.

"You're startin' to look like part of my collection. I'm gonna have to dust you off if you don't move a little." Mrs. Huntemann studied me over her teacup.

"I guess I am a little preoccupied."

"I should wonder." Her shrewd gaze bore into me, and I hooked onto it, like a lifeline. "Terrible thing, death of child. Even worse is the death of a close friend. I've lost both, I know. You don't ever really get over it, but you do survive. Important thing is to feel what you're feeling and *remember*. Too many times people forget. They get busy. They move on. I learned a long time ago there comes a point your memories are all you have. Even if you have to leave behind some of the things you think are important, keep your memories with you. That's why I got all this stuff, helps jog my memory." She smiled, then jabbed a crooked finger toward me. "People die, Emma honey. Memories don't."

I looked away, afraid to tell her I'd effectively killed my memories of Natalie. Mrs. Huntemann smiled and reached over to pat my hand.

"Don't you worry, dearie. Like I said before, sometimes it takes a little time, but you always remember." She set her cup down and rearranged some of the pillows behind her back. "Now I've given you the benefit of an old woman's experience, let's talk about more pressing matters."

"Excuse me?"

"Why the investigation, of course. Those police folks think they know everything about everything and won't listen to a word I have to say, but I figure seeing as how you're an interested party, I can tell you what I know. Maybe together we can get to the truth."

I wasn't sure what to make of her sudden change in attitude. She was all business now, her cheeks flushed with excitement, her hands braced on her knees. I set my cup down and made myself comfortable, wanting to hear her story, but unsure what I could do with the information. And wishing she'd tell me more about how to remember.

"First of all, there's one person I don't think anyone's considered talking to at all. And they should."

"Who?"

"Joyce Slocombe." She said the words in a low voice, slowly and deliberately.

I was confused. Joyce Slocombe had been a counselor with Paulsen Elementary when Natalie and I went there. She was younger than most of the faculty, and wore crisp pantsuits even when the teachers had given up and were coming to school in jeans. She held office hours and presided over competency testing, but I'd never gotten to know her very well. She was always busy, hurrying through the hallways and conferring with teachers. She mostly saw the problem kids, the ones who smoked and wore rock concert t-shirts at age ten. And, of course, I associated her with the state proficiency exams we had to take every year. I'd never enjoyed taking tests and those marathon, multiple-choice monsters gave me hives.

"The school counselor? I don't even think she's still working at Paulsen."

Dorothy's voice returned to normal volume. "No, she's not at the school anymore. She's got her own practice now, up the road in that awful high-rise apartment building. Same one my friend Florence lives in. Ugly monstrosity. Course this place is no Garden of Eden either, I suppose. People don't seem to understand the importance of trees anymore, do they? Cut 'em down one by one and pretty soon there's holes in the very sky above us. Makes no sense. I figure the Afterlife's goin' to be quite a sight after living down here eighty-four years."

She sipped her tea in anticipation. "Where was I? Oh yes, the building where that Joyce works. I pass her door every Thursday when I go up there to visit with Florence. She's gettin' on now, Florence is, doesn't see so well, so I stop by and help her pick up the place, fix a nice lunch, you know. I always bring a casserole so she can just stick it in the oven and heat it up. Makes a nice dinner for her. She won't eat lima beans, though, so I boil 'em awhile till they turn white and tell her they're butter beans. She don't know the difference, and lima beans are good for the eyes.

"Anyway, every time I go I pass by her door. Has a lettered sign on it, 'Joyce Slocombe, Ph.D.'. Sometimes I see the young girls comin' out, red-eyed, blowing their noses. Look so sad. I never took much stock in psychiatrists myself. Seems to me I might's well pay Tinkerbell to listen to my problems. But, then, not everybody likes cats the way I do. Some folks prefer dogs, though what anybody wants with a slobbering animal that can't go to the bathroom without your puttin' it on a leash and walkin' to here and yon twice a day is beyond me."

I was beginning to understand why the police hadn't bothered to take Mrs. Huntemann's statement.

"But what does she have to do with Natalie's death?"

"I don't know. All I said was someone should talk to her. After all, she was here the night the little girl disappeared, and

46

right mad about somethin', too. I saw her storm out of that house with my own eyes and stomp off down the walk with smoke comin' out of her ears. And she didn't go to her car either, she headed for the *creek*." She punctuated this last with a sharp nod.

"From what house? I don't remember her living here."

"No, no, no," Mrs. Huntemann waved a hand in front of her face impatiently, "*She* didn't live here, her friend did. That young black woman...or do they say Afro-American now, I forget. Patricia something. Always wearing love beads and whatnot. That Joyce was over there all the time, she was. Used to park her car in Mr. Freeman's space, not that I minded. Served him right, walkin' all over my daffodils and lettin' his smelly mutt root around my junipers. There's someone couldn't stand cats. I had Clarabelle then. She was Himalayan and just as opinionated as they come. Lived to be nearly nineteen years old, she did. Wouldn't eat liver to save her life. Tinkerbell here loves liver, don't you sweetie?"

Tinkerbell opened her eyes and lifted herself out of the cushions, stretching her body to its full length, which I judged to be about a foot and a half not counting the tail. Then she dropped to the floor, wove her way through the table legs to Mrs. Huntemann's feet and heaved herself onto the couch.

"Well, Clarabelle just hated Mr. Freeman. He'd come by with his brute of a dog and she'd sit in the window hissin' and spittin'. I was afraid to let her out for fear she'd attack the man and he'd sue me or something. He was always callin' the police for some reason or other. I know he had that Joyce's car towed, because I saw it. I was out back watering my azaleas, just mindin' my own business when out he comes, barkin' orders to anyone who'd listen. Threatened to see her in jail if she parked in his space ever again. I'll tell you I was glad when he moved out. Went to Miami the day he retired. I pity the poor old fool who takes his spot at bingo."

Mrs. Huntemann was leaning back with her hand on Tinkerbell's head. The late afternoon sun shot through the drapes and occasional rays of light flew in sparks off her sapphire ring, sending focused beams across the room to ricochet off the ceramic and glass.

I had to admit I was getting drawn into her stories. Mrs Huntemann reminded me of my grandfather. He'd had strong convictions, too. To him, a man who parted his hair in the middle couldn't be trusted, and women who wore fake eyelashes should be horsewhipped. It was hard to argue with him.

"So you think Joyce Slocombe might have some information about the...murder?" I hadn't said the word before now. It brought back the knot in my stomach. Full force.

"Could be. Won't know unless we ask, now, will we?"

I got the feeling the "we" she was talking about was me. I wasn't sure how I'd suddenly gotten roped into detective work, but I had to admit she had a point. If the police wouldn't listen to her, they wouldn't know to question Joyce Slocombe.

"Patrice! That's it. Her friend's name was Patrice. Patrice Carroll. Sometimes it takes me awhile, but I always remember." She settled back into the cushions satisfied with herself once again.

I didn't expect to recognize this new name. Patrice Carroll was well-known in the gay community for her work with the Gay & Lesbian Rights Council and the Black Lesbians' Political Caucus. Carly had worked with Pat on several projects and was currently helping plan a fund-raiser for the GLRC. Carly idolized Pat Carroll. Somehow, knowing Joyce and Patrice had probably been lovers made me want to talk to Joyce even more.

I leaned forward, wanting to hear more of what Mrs. Huntemann had to say. "What else do you think the police are missing?"

"Besides the sense God gave 'em and a little humility? I doubt they know the girl's father was here that night."

"Frank Mercer? You saw him?"

"I did. He had on one of those olive green army coats that has all the pockets in it. You know, the kind that poofs out in all directions?" She puffed her cheeks and held her arms out to her sides, looking for all the world like a blue snowman, then continued. "I remember because it was dark out and I was taking a walk with Clarabelle. I saw him through the corner of my eye, you know, and to me it looked like *he* was carryin' a cat, too. Turned out it was just one of his pockets turned inside out, but for all the world I thought it was a cat. You know how sometimes your eyes can play little tricks on you? I'll never forget one time I swore there was a bunny rabbit in my backyard. I stood at the window, still as can be, not breathing for fear I'd scare it off. When it didn't move for a while, I took a chance and slid the glass door open bit by bit. Well, I got it open and stepped out onto the patio, inching closer and closer...and guess what?"

"What?"

"It was a leaf. Just a plain old leaf dried brown and crinkled into the shape of a bunny rabbit. I laughed myself silly. I'll have to remember to tell my eye doctor that one next time I go."

Mrs. Huntemann was tilting a little to one side against the pillows, patting the cat each time she laughed. I was laughing, too, at her story and at the look on Tinkerbell's face every time Mrs. Huntemann's hand came down on her head. She looked like she was dribbling the cat down court for a lay-up.

"Did you talk to Natalie's father?"

"Oh heavens, no. I started towards him, thinkin' he was carrying a cat and all, but when he saw me he just whipped around and headed down the drive. Guess he wasn't much for talking. And of course when I realized it wasn't a cat after all, but his pocket turned inside-out, I figured I wouldn't have much to say to him anyway."

I doubted Mrs. Huntemann would ever have trouble finding something to say.

"What was he doing here?"

"Watchin' the house like he always did, I suppose. He used to come here all the time. Stand by the side of your house across

49

the way, he would, and stare up into the little girl's room. I never saw him go in, he'd just stand there and watch. Felt kind of sorry for him, I did, not getting to see his little girl and all. Especially after that lawyer moved in. Seemed her father was around here a lot more after that, I suppose because he didn't get to spend as much time with the girl."

I felt I needed to assure Mrs. Huntemann that Natalie wasn't missing much. "He wasn't a very positive influence on her."

"Oh I know he drank and they'd had some rough times, that family, but it doesn't take away from a father's love for his little girl. My father used to say to me, 'Dorothy, I may yell and I may scream and sometimes I may have to take the strap to you, but it doesn't mean I don't love you and it doesn't mean I wouldn't move a mountain for you if you wanted me to.' I guess just knowing he would, I never thought to ask." She shrugged her shoulders and sighed, smiling to herself and shaking her head side to side.

My grandfather had been the closest thing to a father to me. After he died, I made do without one. I never questioned having just one parent, but listening to Mrs. Huntemann's memories of her father, I was beginning to believe I'd missed something.

We talked a little while longer, and I learned how bone china is made, why cats prefer the color yellow to any other, and that Mrs. Huntemann had once been a regular guest of Rosalyn and Jimmy Carter.

When I finally looked at my watch, it was nearly 7:30. As much as I wanted to stay and talk, I needed to get home. As I took one last look around the room, I wished I'd been able to appreciate Mrs. Huntemann more when I'd lived so close, that she could have been more in my young life than an endless source of chocolate. I gave her a long hug and promised I wouldn't be a stranger, vowing to myself to keep the promise. She slipped into the kitchen and came back with a paper plate heaped with brownies and covered in plastic wrap. I thanked her and left both my own and my mother's address and phone number.

Before leaving, I made the mistake of planting a kiss on Tinkerbell's misused head. She shot me a look that chills my spine to this day.

Chapter 7

We were huddled under the blanket in our fort, having climbed up the slippery concrete steps in the rain. Natalie's hair hung in damp strands that clung to her neck and shoulders. I was shivering, rubbing my arms for warmth and wishing we had another blanket. I wasn't looking forward to climbing back down.

"Guess what I saw?" Natalie held a Barbie doll in one hand and was combing its hair with a tiny pink plastic comb.

"What?" My teeth had begun chattering. I wrapped my arms around my knees and leaned farther into the corner.

"Miss Slocombe. Kissing somebody." She didn't look up, but continued pulling the comb through the doll's matted nylon hair.

"Kissing who?"

"Guess."

I buried my cheeks between my knees, blowing hot air into the gap and rocking slightly back and forth. "Mr. White?"

"Nope."

"That new teacher, the bald one?"

"Nope."

"Well, who?"

"Somebody that lives at the end of our row."

"Somebody *here*?" I mentally counted the houses in our row, dismissing neighbors one by one on the basis of marriage, age and whether I thought I could ever kiss them.

"Not Mr. Freeman?"

"No, Yuck!" Natalie's face screwed up in distaste. "Somebody else."

"Who?"

Her eyes met mine and sparkled in the dim corner of the fort. "Miss Carroll."

"The black lady? No way, you're lying."

She looked hurt and angry. "I am not! I saw it. They were in Miss Carroll's living room and the curtains were open and I walked by just when they started kissing."

"Really? They weren't just hugging?"

"Nope. They were kissing. With lips."

"Yeah, but my mom kisses your mom sometimes."

"It wasn't like that. It was real long, and they had their eyes closed." Natalie closed her eyes and puckered her lips to illustrate. "Miss Slocombe saw me, too. She ran over and closed the curtains. She looked really mad."

We sat in silence for a moment, considering this exciting news. I tried to picture Miss Slocombe and Miss Carroll kissing, but I kept seeing me and Natalie. "I didn't know grown-up girls kissed."

Natalie went back to combing Barbie's hair. "Sure they do. All the time. And besides, Miss Slocombe and Miss Carroll are getting married."

"Girls can't get married!" This I was sure of.

"Sure they can. That's why they were kissing. Miss Carroll gave Miss Slocombe a wedding ring and then they kissed."

Suddenly I could actually see Natalie and me living in our house with the swimming pool and the canopy bed.

"But who'll be the husband?" I wanted to know everything. I wanted Natalie to be right.

"Nobody, stupid. Your mom doesn't have a husband, right?"

Butterflies churned inside my stomach. I felt just like I had the day Natalie first kissed me. I watched her yanking the comb through the doll's hair and wished she'd kiss me again, now. I didn't know how to ask.

Natalie looked up, crinkling her forehead into a question mark. Her eyes grew dark and the smile faded from her lips.

I knew she was thinking hard about something. "Natalie, what's wrong?"

"I was just wondering how old you have to be to get married."

Chapter 8

Needless to say, I didn't sleep well Saturday night. Going back to Oakbrook had helped to release some of my memories of Natalie, but they were jumbled, some clearer than others, some just fleeting images, some frightening in their emotional intensity. I lay in bed trying to sort them out, knowing I was obsessing, reading a lot more into my feelings for Natalie than I should. After all, we were only eight years old. But a part of me truly felt as if I had lost a lover.

Finally I fell into a restless sleep, dreaming of Natalie and Judy. Their faces faded in and out of focus, sometimes blending together, Natalie's white-blonde hair curling up at the ends and darkening into Judy's short brown curls. Then Judy's penetrating grey eyes would dissolve into sky-blue, the pupils still pulsating with sensual heat.

In another dream, I watched Natalie climb the terrace, resolutely picking her way up the concrete slabs and calling to me to follow. Then she became Judy, waving goodbye to me from an airport escalator. I tried to run and catch up to Judy, weaving among weary travelers weighted down with luggage until I reached the bottom of the escalator. I stepped on and began to walk up, only to find I was back at Oakbrook, climbing the terrace.

Natalie screamed "Don't look down!" I glanced over my shoulder, feeling the cold concrete digging into my palms. I was too high, my fingers slipping. Natalie called to me, scrambling down to help me. Then I heard a deafening crack as the step Natalie was standing on gave way, one end crushing into the step beneath. Natalie fell in slow motion past me, landing on her back on the floor of the ravine. She didn't move.

A figure materialized over her body, touching a sensuous hand to her forehead. I could see each finger clearly, long and graceful, as they moved over Natalie's skin. Then the figure turned, looking up at me—blaming me. It was Bobbie.

I woke drenched in cold sweat, gripping the edge of the bed and gasping for air. Sun streamed through my window, casting bright bars of light on the ceiling. My legs were tangled in the covers, my nightshirt twisted around my waist, biting into my skin. I sat up and buried my head in my hands, rubbing the sleep from my eyes. With one hand braced against the cool wall, I padded to the bathroom and splashed icy water on my face, drinking greedily from a cupped palm.

After a long, hot shower, I felt better, but the dream still played in my mind. I fixed a cup of strong tea and sat on the couch, staring blankly at the newspaper on the table in front of me. Unfolding it quickly, I darted through the headlines on the front page, expecting to see something about Natalie. But there was nothing there. I should have been relieved, but it just made me angry. How could life, people, events go on when a child had been killed? And not just any child, but Natalie.

Natalie.

She wasn't coming back.

I stared for a few moments at a picture of two small children squatting near the edge of a pond. They were reaching out, tossing torn pieces of bread at a mean-looking swan. The caption read, "Stacy and Jennifer Brandon, 8 and 9, feed the birds at Claridge Park. Saturday's summer sun brought local residents out in force to picnic and play at area parks. More sunny weather forecasted, page B2." The picture filled half the page. Twice as much space as they'd given to Natalie.

I leaned back, planting my feet on the edge of the coffee table, and kicked the paper onto the floor.

Some Sunday.

Normally, Sunday morning is my favorite time of the week. I look forward to it, a time I can sit in silence and regenerate. I put on music, then spread the paper out on the floor and read it section by section, starting with the front page and ending with the color supplements. It's my time for me.

This morning I wasn't up to it. I felt restless, confined behind the broad windows of my apartment. The venetian blinds in the living room hovered about six inches above the sill, and I could see heat waves rippling off the roof of the apartment building next door. I wanted to be outside, letting the fresh air clear my mind. I wanted to talk to someone.

I set the tea, still hot, on the coffee table and grabbed my canvas bag and the suit Mom had loaned me, thinking I'd drop by and spend a little time watching her pull weeds in the backyard.

* * * * *

That's how I found myself back in my old neighborhood, steering the Celica aimlessly through the familiar streets. I'd driven by Mom's house, but her silver Buick was already gone from the driveway. Now I was just driving, the windows down, my fingers tapping the steering wheel as Sinead O'Connor pulsed from the stereo speakers.

More memories came back to me. I smiled as I passed the drug store Natalie and I had robbed when we were seven. It hadn't changed, although it was now anchor to a mini-mall with startling yellow signs advertising a dry cleaner, a card shop and a windowless Chinese Restaurant.

It was on a dare, our infamous heist. A boy in the complex, showing us a shoebox full of stolen candy bars and comic books, had bet we couldn't do it, and Natalie had taken the challenge for both of us.

We walked the four blocks to the drug store looking over our shoulders all the way. Outside, we stood against the wall planning our strategy, whispering and looking up every time a customer passed. Finally we went in. We separated inside, Natalie roaming through the aisles, occasionally picking up a bottle of shampoo or a can of cat food and pretending to read the label. I was blind with panic. I stood flipping the pages of a magazine—I think it was *Popular Mechanics*—and watching her in the convex mirror at the far corner of the store.

Eventually she reached the candy bins. She stood in front of them for what seemed like hours, shifting her weight from foot to foot and glancing periodically at the cashier. Then, when he turned away to speak to the pharmacist, she grabbed three bags of M&Ms and shoved them in her pocket.

Shaking with fear, I dropped the magazine. I jumped at the sound and heard the cashier bellow, "Hey, kid! Put it back or buy it!" I slammed it back in the rack and raced for the door. I kept running till I'd crossed the street and was safely hidden behind a hedge. Through the dusty leaves, I watched the store for several minutes, sure they had arrested Natalie. I glanced nervously up and down the street, listening for sirens, expecting at any moment for a hand to clamp down on my shoulder. Then Natalie walked out of the store, a Cheshire grin on her face and her hand still in her pocket.

I was so sure we'd get caught that I made her throw the M&Ms down a storm drain. We never convinced the boy we'd actually done it, and we never tried it again. A few weeks later, my mother and I went to the store. I insisted on waiting in the car, which she couldn't understand, then when she came out, she'd bought me some M&Ms. I told her the whole story. She marched me back into the store and made me apologize to the manager. Then she grounded me for two weeks.

I couldn't remember if Natalie got in trouble.

After putting a few dozen unnecessary miles on the Celica driving in circles, I found myself pulling into the parking lot of Joyce Slocombe's building.

The building was new. I counted seven stories and guessed there were about ten apartments on each floor. Low bushes bordered a sloping garden in front, where agapanthus grew in symmetrical rows, snowballs of trumpet-shaped flowers in blue and purple weighing down the succulent stems.

I walked into the air-conditioned lobby and approached the building directory. Joyce Slocombe's name appeared under "Business" in Suite 710 and "Residents" in Suite 711.

I glanced at my watch. It was nearly 11:00, so I decided to take a chance she was at home. I assumed she wouldn't have any appointments on Sunday. Riding up in the mirrored elevator, I tucked in my shirt and ignored my hair, trying in vain not to listen to an instrumental version of "Staying Alive" that whined through a speaker in the wall. Walking down the deserted hallway, I found her office door first, labelled just as Mrs. Huntemann had described it, but I continued down the hall and knocked softly on 711.

If she'd been more than five feet away from the door, I know she wouldn't have heard me, but she opened the door almost immediately. An empty coffee mug dangled from her free hand. It was printed with an academic seal that read "Psychotic State."

Joyce didn't speak at once, but raised her eyebrows in a pleasant, questioning way.

"Yes? Can I help you?"

She looked exactly as I remembered her, and suddenly I felt eight years old again. I realized I had no idea what I was going to say to her.

"I'm...My name is Emma Kendrick. You used to be the counselor at my elementary school. I was just...." I faltered and stopped.

She frowned a little and cocked her head to one side, looking at me more closely. Just when I was sure she was going to shut the door in my face, she opened it wider and moved to one side.

"Come in, Emma. Can I get you a cup of coffee? I was just fixing one for myself."

She gestured with the mug toward the kitchen.

"Sure. With cream. Thank you." I felt like a moron. What was I doing here? I cursed myself for getting caught up in Mrs. Huntemann's stories.

She returned with a steaming mug in each hand and indicated we should sit. Setting a cup on the oak coffee table in front of me, she sat in a round basket chair on the other side and crossed her legs. She watched me silently, sipping her coffee.

I wrapped my hands around the warm cup and spoke directly into the creamy liquid. It smelled like cinnamon.

"I'm not sure why I'm here exactly, I...I was a friend of Natalie Campbell's. She died.... They found her...."

My voice sank beneath the coffee's swirling surface.

"That's all right. Take your time."

Her voice was soothing, low and fluid. I glanced up and saw she was tilting her head slightly, her short blonde hair fanning out from the side of her head over her ear.

She'd hardly aged. She was still slender, with bare muscular arms in a white t-shirt with the short cuffs rolled, and a pair of camel slacks. A thin gold chain circling her neck caught the light, rising and falling each time she took a breath. Without make-up, her skin was clear and unwrinkled, her brown eyes intense beneath sandy brows. She held her coffee cup around the bowl, her fingers threaded through the useless handle.

I scanned the room, strangely unable to look at her. Instead I focused on a painting directly behind Joyce's left shoulder that portrayed a woman's nude body melting into the shape of an orchid.

I took a deep breath and tried again.

"I guess I'm here because I remember you from Paulsen.... I was over at Oakbrook yesterday, talking with Dorothy Huntemann. She lives there. She said you were there—at the complex—the night Natalie disappeared...that you used to go there to visit Patrice Carroll...."

I knew I wasn't making any sense, but Joyce seemed to be

following me anyway.

"I see. I remember Mrs. Huntemann. And she's right, I did go there to visit Patrice. We were lovers."

I didn't know whether to look surprised. Her expression hadn't changed. She still watched me, sipping her coffee, relaxed and waiting.

"Does that bother you?"

"No, I mean...I guess I knew that. Natalie said she saw—I mean, I know Patrice is very active in the gay community...." I took a long sip of coffee that burned my tongue and throat going down.

"Are you a lesbian?"

"Yes, I am."

"I see.... Do you have a lover?"

I focused on the watercolor of the orchid-woman, thinking Judy would have loved it. She loved natural imagery and believed fervently in the fundamental connection between women and nature.

"No. We separated five months ago. She moved to Oregon."

"I'm sorry to hear that. Ending relationships can be difficult. Was she your first lover?"

"Not the first, but the most important."

"You must miss her."

The coffee didn't burn as much the second time around, but it settled in my stomach like liquor, sending waves of heat flooding through my already searing veins. I nodded weakly.

"Tell me about her."

Judy, in shredded jeans rolled to the knees, waded through a tide pool across the room. Bent over, she turned her face to me and grinned. In her eyes, the light reflecting off the water became fire.

"She was...I mean, she *is* an ornithologist. In training, I guess. She works with endangered species. Mostly sea birds. Counts them. That kind of thing."

"Yes, but what is she like?"

61

"I don't know...." I could see Judy sitting at her desk chewing on a pencil as she studied some papers from work as if she were there in the room. She pushed her glasses up on her nose and winked at me. "She's very committed. She knows what she wants. I mean, she's caring. She's very supportive. But she doesn't have a lot of patience, I guess. She never really understood people who didn't just go out and get what they want...."

"People?"

I looked up, not sure what I'd been saying. Judy's face, paled by the harsh desk lamp, resolved itself into Joyce's sunlit, angular features. We were talking about Judy...but why? I couldn't remember.

"Excuse me?"

"You were saying your lover didn't understand 'people' who don't get what they want. Were you one of those people?"

"I guess so...I was working as a secretary at this publishing firm and they kept saying they'd promote me, but they never did. She thought I should give them an ultimatum."

"And did you?"

"I didn't have to. They finally promoted me.... The week after Judy left."

She nodded, her eyes soft with sympathy.

"That must have been an emotional time for you."

"Yeah, I guess it was. I just kept wishing Judy could have been there, you know? I kept thinking maybe it would have made a difference."

She didn't say anything. I felt suddenly exposed, vulnerable. How had I started talking about Judy? About everything I'd been feeling when she left? I'd never talked about it before. I tried with Carly right after Judy left, but she was so busy blaming Judy and dragging me to museums and on bike rides that I gave up. Now everything was just pouring out. I wanted to stop, and yet I didn't.

Joyce smiled at me, as if she could tell what I was thinking. Then her eyes focused on a point behind me and she seemed to retreat into a world of her own.

62

"Patrice was my first lover. I didn't know until I met her that I was a lesbian. She opened up a whole new world for me. Helped me discover a strength and confidence in myself that I'd never known I had. She was a very strong woman—still is. Very independent. Very honest. In the end, I suppose that's what destroyed our relationship."

"How?" She could have been describing Judy, and I longed to know how she had gotten over Patrice. I still woke some mornings expecting to feel Judy's warm, soft body beside mine. When she first left, I'd set aside enough money to buy a plane ticket to Portland, sure she'd call and beg me to come. When she didn't, I'd used the money to buy a leather jacket. It was vindictive in a way, Judy was a strict vegetarian who wouldn't even wear wool.

Joyce ignored my question. "Why did she go to Oregon?"

"Judy? She got a job offer with an environmental group. It was a really good job, I guess she couldn't pass it up."

"And that ended your relationship? Her moving?"

"Well, we'd been having a hard time. We'd been together over two years and I guess the romance was gone. Breaking up made the most sense."

"I see." She watched me, expecting me to continue.

I decided I had to get to the point. My heart was burning with the pain that thinking about Judy always dredged up. Ever since Natalie's body had been uncovered, I'd been thinking about Judy a lot more than I wanted to. I needed to get a grip on myself. Joyce was a sympathetic listener, but I'd come for a reason. I dove in.

"Anyway, as I said, I talked to Mrs. Huntemann yesterday and she said you were at the complex that night. I just thought...I mean, the police wouldn't talk to Mrs. Huntemann, so they probably don't know you were there, and I thought maybe you would want...I mean, if you saw anything that night, maybe it would help them find out who...why Natalie disappeared."

"You mean who killed her."

That did it. The coffee cup shook in my hands as I set it back on the table. I pressed my fingers against the bridge of my nose to quell the tears rising behind my eyes and took a deep breath, willing myself to calm down. I counted to ten, listening to my heart beating double time in my chest. Gradually it slowed and I opened my eyes, rubbing my hands together and locking them in my lap. Joyce reached over and placed a box of tissues in front of me.

"You must be having some very strong feelings right now. I read an article in the paper about her remains being found. Were you very close?"

"She was my best friend."

Joyce set her mug on the coffee table and sat up straight, smoothing her slacks with both hands and then resting them on her knees. "I remember Natalie. She was a beautiful child. I believe her parents were divorced?"

"Yes. Her mother remarried when she was four."

"That's right, Robert Campbell. I recognized the name in the paper. Natalie was a bright child, although as I recall she was suffering emotionally."

"She was?" I couldn't remember Natalie ever being sad, and I'd never seen her cry. Or had I? Why couldn't I remember?

"As I recall, she'd been referred to me by her teacher at one point. Her grades had been falling and her teacher seemed to think it might have something to do with Natalie adjusting to her mother's second marriage."

I tried to remember Natalie ever talking about that. My mother and I had gone to Angela and Robert's wedding. Natalie was the flower girl, wearing a gossamer yellow dress with five starched petticoats. She'd danced up the aisle, tossing white rose petals at everyone she knew. When the ceremony began, she jumped up from the front pew and ran back to sit with me. All the guests—even Robert and Angela—had laughed. She'd been happy all day.

"I don't think she had any trouble. She liked Robert...." I

sounded doubtful. I felt resentful that suddenly Joyce seemed to know more about Natalie than I did. I pressed on.

"So you met with Natalie? In your office?"

Joyce chuckled.

I frowned, wondering what she found so funny.

"I'm sorry," she said. "It's just the way you said that. 'My office.' I remember there was quite a mystique about my office at Paulsen. Even the teachers didn't want to be seen in there. I don't know why, I guess they thought if they went in, everyone would think they were insane. The principal used to come by, knock on my door and refuse to come in. We'd hold meetings in the hallway. And the children, oh! The looks on their faces when I'd lead them inside. I think they expected thumb screws and live wires. I finally had to get rid of the couch, no one would go near it."

She smiled, shaking her head.

"But what about Natalie?"

"Well, I did talk with her a few times. We should have met more, but she resisted my help as I remember. From what little I learned, I suspected she was being abused."

The phone rang and Joyce excused herself to answer it. My mind was reeling, trying to make sense of what she'd said. All I could think about was a girl I'd known in high school, Kathy, who was abused. She wasn't a close friend, but we talked occasionally. After I'd known her a few months I began to realize she was nearly always wearing a bandage or a cast on some part of her body. I asked her about it the day she showed up in a full leg cast after Thanksgiving break. Kathy said she'd fallen down a flight of stairs and joked about being accident prone. Later that year someone notified the police. They looked into it and found out both her parents had been systematically beating Kathy and her younger brother for years. They went to live with their grandparents for a while, but the next year she was back in school and living with her parents again.

I came upon Kathy in the locker room once. She was undressed except for her bra and panties. Her back and thighs were covered with scars, one of which had clearly been caused by a hot iron pressed and held against her shoulder.

Could that have happened to Natalie? Everything in me denied it was possible—and yet it had taken years for anyone to discover what Kathy had suffered. Could she have hidden it? If only I could remember.

Joyce returned and picked up the coffee cups. "I'm sorry, Emma, I'm afraid I have to go out for awhile. Why don't you write your address and phone number on the pad by the door. I'd like us to keep in touch. I'm interested to hear what becomes of the investigation."

Still dazed, I wrote out the information without even seeing the paper in front of me. At the door, I turned back to say goodbye. Joyce was standing by the coffee table with the same studied look on her face she'd had when I first arrived.

"I'm sorry this is so difficult on you, Emma. I wish we could have talked longer. I'll call you later on to see how you're doing."

"Thank you." I shut the door behind me and stood in the hallway, bracing an arm against the wall for support. My knees were weak, and I couldn't get the image of Kathy's burned shoulder out of my mind.

Chapter 9

Natalie was late for school. At recess, I sat on a stone bench near the playground, watching fresh-faced girls in bright dresses and colorful tights swinging on the monkeybars. My gaze shifted often to the grassy field behind them, scanning for Natalie to push her way through the fence.

Squeals of delight filled the air, and I watched as one of the girls threw her dirty white sweater over a short metal bar and swung a leg on top of it. She hopped once, wrapping her plump arms around the bent leg, and began to swing her body back and forth. Soon, she was twirling around the bar in circles, her long red hair dragging along the ground and then flying out behind her and slapping against her back as she rounded the top of the bar. Her friends clapped and cheered, standing back to avoid her free leg as it whipped past them during a turn.

A flash of light caught my eye and I looked toward the school to see Natalie emerging from one of the building's glass-fronted doors. She walked slowly toward me, her head down, one arm bent and held close to her body. I waited for her to reach me, moving over to make room on the bench for her to sit.

"Hi. Where were you?"

She sat down and turned to watch the girls on the playground, her eyes clouded and her face blank.

"Natalie? Where were you?"

She didn't look at me when she answered. "I didn't feel good, so my mom let me sleep in. She drove me to school."

"What's wrong? Are you sick?"

"No." She was wearing a red sweater over a yellow tee shirt and jeans. Occasionally she plucked at the left sleeve of her sweater, her arm lying limp in her lap.

"Aren't you hot?" It was early October, and the sun floated big and hot in a cloudless sky. Several groups of children sat near the building, leaning against the wall in the shade of the roof. I straddled the bench, my sandals hanging off my toes and fanning the soles of my feet.

Natalie looked at me, unsmiling. Slowly, she shrugged her right arm out of the sweater, revealing a gauze bandage that covered the length of her forearm.

"What happened?" I touched the bandage carefully, lifting her arm to see the tape that encircled it and held the bandage in place.

"I fell. Mom took me to the doctor this morning. He said I just scraped it." She placed her right hand on the bandage and pulled the arm closer to her chest. I could see an ugly bruise forming on her wrist.

"How?" It looked like it hurt her a lot.

"I just fell. I scraped it on the floor. It's no big deal." Her gaze returned to the playground.

The same red-headed girl was now sitting atop a taller bar, bracing her hands against the metal on either side of her body. Suddenly, she dropped backward, flinging her body out and landing unsteadily on her feet in front of the bar. The crowd cheered.

Natalie didn't come to the terrace after school. That night I heard her window scrape open and I sat up in bed to look out my window. "Where were you?"

"My arm hurt too much to climb."

I don't remember what else we talked about, but at least I felt glad things were okay between us. Then the door to her room opened, the dim light from the hall making her pink curtains glow orange. She turned away from me to see who it was, then turned back. The moonlight shimmered off her hair, and for a second I could have sworn I saw a tear roll down her cheek. But Natalie never cried.

She didn't say anything to me, but slowly closed the window and ducked beneath the curtain.

Chapter 10

I got home from visiting Joyce around four o'clock, tired and even more confused than I had been when I left. I dropped my canvas bag on the floor and collapsed onto the couch, glad I wasn't going to work for a few days, but dreading the memorial service Monday morning.

I lay motionless on the couch, my head resting on folded arms, and tried not to think about child abuse. Once my mother had gotten mad at me and threatened me with a trowel. She was on the patio at Oakbrook, down on her knees transplanting some seedlings. I bounded through the sliding-glass doors and upset a bag of potting soil, spilling it all over the concrete. I'd startled her, and she jumped up, holding the trowel in front of my face. She was angrier than I'd ever seen her. The trowel shook in her hand.

"Don't you ever, *ever* run up behind me like that again, do you understand me?" Her cheeks were red and her eyes blazed at me. For some reason, I found it funny. I started to laugh.

She made a throaty, growling sound and raised the trowel.

"Don't laugh at me, young lady!"

But by this time, I couldn't stop.

Her arm jerked back and I ducked, screaming "Mommy, no!"

She stopped instantly and stared at me, disbelieving. Then in a single motion, she fell to her knees and pulled me toward her. She was crying, her face buried in my shoulder. She begged me to forgive her. I wrapped my arms around her neck and tried to soothe her, patting the back of her head. It was the closest she had ever come to hitting me.

Later she told me that was the day she found out my grandfather had cancer.

I opened my eyes and stared at the stitching on the back of the sofa. I'll never understand how a parent—anyone—could hit a child, let alone suffer a child to endure what my friend Kathy had been through. I lifted my head and turned to face the room, breathing in the cool air and saying a silent prayer for her.

The red light on my answering machine blinked every few seconds. I watched it hypnotically, counting the pauses between each blink. It reminded me of the times I'd stayed in bed watching lightning flash across my ceiling, waiting for the thunder to reach me. Blink. One-one thousand, two-one thousand, three—blink. I heaved myself up and went over to the desk, punching the rewind button and walking into the kitchen.

"Hey, Dil-Emma, what's up? Just calling to let you know that you, yes *you*, have been chosen in very close race, by the *slightest* of margins, to help me stuff envelopes tonight for the GLuRCk fund-raiser. This is a high honor I wouldn't bestow on just anyone, you understand, but after consulting my handlers and numerous business and civic leaders, we've decided you're the right person for the job. In return, I'll pick up some of that repulsive orange chicken you like from the Beijing Garden. Five-thirty okay? You're the best!"

The message ended with Carly making kissing sounds.

I looked around my apartment, satisfied it was clean enough for Carly. I've lived alone ever since Judy left, and I've gotten to appreciate the solitude. My apartment is fairly large—Judy and I used to share it—one bedroom with a spacious kitchen and two walk-in closets. I've furnished it a little at a time, gradually replacing the pieces Judy took with her and the old things my mother gave me when I got out of college. The sofa is beige and folds out into a bed, with a coffee table and bookcases in wood veneer. Not terribly colorful, but then neither am I. I do have a

71

beautiful quilt my great-grandmother made on the bed. And the walls are covered with old movie and theatrical posters, some in frames, some dry-mounted onto foam-core. I like to think of it as Early Post-Feminist. Carly says it reminds her of a dentist's waiting room.

I picked up a few discarded pieces of clothing and threw them in the hamper, checking to see that there was enough toilet paper left on the roll. If I've learned anything from my mother, I've learned you never allow a guest into your home without checking the toilet paper supply.

Carly came through the door at 6:15 loaded down with boxes of envelopes and flyers and a greasy bag of Chinese food. She plopped everything on the table and sank into a chair, exhaling dramatically.

"I had to park two blocks away. What is it with this place, doesn't anyone ever leave? The parking lot's completely full."

"I'm sure there were plenty of spaces forty-five minutes ago." I gave her a knowing look and took the bag of Chinese food into the kitchen. I set it on the counter, pulling out the little white boxes and sniffing them cautiously to see what was inside.

"I know, I know, I know. I was just heading out the door when Jill called." Carly moved the boxes of envelopes to the floor and stood in the kitchen doorway. "She's getting together a group to go see Kate Clinton at the Brewster Auditorium. Wanna go?"

I pulled two plates out of the cupboard and handed them to Carly. "When?"

"The sixteenth. She said Kay and Marty want to go, and probably Linda. We could go for pizza afterwards."

"Sure." I brought the food to the table and handed Carly a spoon, reaching for the orange chicken box.

"Good, I already told her yes." Carly smiled mischievously, dishing sweet and sour shrimp onto her plate. "You look like hell, by the way, what's up?"

"I guess I'm still upset about Natalie."

"Oh, yeah. Listen, I'm sorry I wasn't very supportive the other night."

"That's okay. I'm just tired. I'm taking a few days off work, that should help." I dug into a pile of fried rice and tried not to notice Carly staring at me across the table.

She studied me in silence for a few minutes. "You know, you shouldn't let this get to you so much. I mean, I know it's a shock and everything, but there's nothing you can do."

"I know. My mom said the same thing. I just feel, I don't know, like I should be doing something. 'Avenging her death' or something. I don't know." I looked at the orange chicken longingly, but I'd lost my appetite. I changed the subject.

"I met one of Pat Carroll's former lovers today." That got Carly's attention. She smiled.

"You'd have to be in solitary not to."

"Carly!"

"I'm just kidding. Actually, I'm just jealous. I wouldn't mind fixing her breakfast in bed one of these days..."

"Really? Don't tell me Carly Velasquez, confirmed bachelorette, is finally in love?"

"Love, no. Lust, quite possibly. Wait till you meet her, you'll know what I'm talking about."

"Actually, I have met her, in a way. She lived at Oakbrook when Natalie and I did."

"Small world. So which Lucky Bitch did you meet?"

"Her name's Joyce Slocombe. She was a counselor at the school Natalie and I went to. She's in private practice now in Arlington."

"How'd you meet her?" She was shovelling in the food with characteristic vigor. Carly has worn a size five since she was in ninth grade, but she eats like a linebacker.

"I went to her apartment. It's a long story. I went to Oakbrook yesterday and I ran into this old woman, Mrs. Huntemann—"

"Ageist comment, Ms. Kendrick. Watch yourself."

"You're right, sorry. This *woman,* Mrs. Huntemann, who lived there when Natalie and I did. She told me Joyce was at the complex the night Natalie disappeared. So I went to see if she had talked to the police yet."

"You what?!!" She choked down a mouthful of shrimp and fried rice and chugged some water. "Jesus, Emma, since when are you Nancy Drew? Why did you go to Oakbrook in the first place?"

"I don't know. I had some crazy idea I would remember more about Natalie if I went back to where we lived." I got up and placed my plate, still half-full, in the sink, sorry I had mentioned Joyce at all.

"This thing is really getting to you, isn't it?"

I leaned against the counter and pressed a hand to my forehead. "Yeah, I guess so. It's just that I keep trying and I can't remember half the things we did. I mean, we were together all the time and yet I can't remember what we did. I get these little bits and pieces, you know? But mostly it's just a blank."

"Come on, Emma, you were just a kid. Nobody remembers everything they did when they were eight years old. Hell, I don't even remember *being* eight years old." She turned away and started picking up the boxes of Chinese food off the table. "You have to let this go. Somebody *killed* her, Emma. Let the police find out who."

She handed me the boxes and I opened the refrigerator, stacking them on the top shelf and letting the air from inside cool my face.

"But they're *not* doing it, Carly. They wouldn't even talk to Mrs. Huntemann and she said she saw both Joyce and Natalie's father there the night she disappeared."

I closed the refrigerator door and followed Carly into the living room, picking up a box of flyers from the dining room floor.

Carly sat on the floor and opened a box of envelopes. "Natalie's father? Isn't he some big lawyer or something?"

"No, that's her stepfather. Her father's name is Frank Mercer. Natalie's mother divorced him when she was two. He's an alcoholic."

"Oh, terrific. Sounds like a peach of a guy. So what are you going to do, pound down his door and demand to know what he was doing on February 14th at 11:30 p.m.?" Carly grabbed a stack of fliers and started folding them into thirds.

"No...I just wanted to talk to Joyce and see if the police had questioned her yet." I resented Carly's attitude. I wanted her to understand what I was feeling, but I wasn't getting through.

"Well, had they?"

"I don't know. I don't think so. She was sort of evasive. She kept asking me about Judy."

"Judy?" Carly spat her name. "What does she have to do with anything?"

"I don't know. Just that when Joyce started talking about Patrice and then she asked if I had a lover... She was really nice, Carly, it seemed like she really... I don't know. Understood." I concentrated on folding a flier, not wanting to look at Carly.

"That's what shrinks do, Emma. They get you to tell them all your problems without ever revealing anything about themselves." She sounded disgusted.

I looked up and saw she was staring at me. She looked almost hurt.

"I know. I just...it felt good having someone to talk to. I've got a lot on my mind and it seemed like she was willing to listen."

"Sure, for fifty bucks an hour." Carly went back to folding fliers, throwing the folded ones into a pile between us.

I wasn't sure why Carly was being so negative about therapy, but I knew I didn't want to talk about it anymore. Carly and I rarely argue, probably because I always try to avoid the subjects on which we don't agree. I made a mental note to add therapy to the list.

The wall of folded flyers grew silently larger between us.

"I'm going to turn on the news. See if the police have any leads yet."

I got up and flicked on the TV on my way to the bathroom. Closing the door, I stood in front of the mirror with my palms against my cheeks. I felt hot and angry with Carly for not understanding. She's never been a bedrock of emotional support—I count on her more to entertain me than to help me analyze my feelings. But I wanted her support now. I rinsed a washcloth under the tap and wiped my face, letting the wet cotton cool my skin.

When I came out, Carly had moved and was leaning against the coffee table, stuffing the folded fliers into envelopes. She looked up and raised her eyebrows in appeal.

"I'm sorry, Em, I didn't mean to get you upset."

I sat down beside her and pulled a box of envelopes closer. "That's okay. I'm sorry I got upset."

"You can talk to *me* about all this, you know."

"I know. It's just, sometimes I think no one can understand. I don't even understand it."

"It'll be okay. It just takes time." She squeezed my hand and went back to stuffing envelopes.

The news had just begun, the top story a five-car pile-up on the beltway. I watched in silence, tensing each time the anchor concluded a report and began another.

I had just about given up on hearing anything about Natalie when a graphic of a magnifying glass and an enlarged fingerprint appeared behind the anchor's shoulder. The caption read "INVESTIGATION."

"Police reported no new leads today in the investigation of the death of eight-year-old Natalie Campbell. But our own Kevin Johnson reports Natalie's mother, Angela Campbell, was once the target of child abuse allegations. Kevin?"

"My God." Carly took my hand and held it in her lap.

The field reporter stood on the gravel drive outside the Campbell's home. The striped drapes in the massive window were drawn.

"It was in 1968, but some police officials think a one-page report filed with the county's Human Services Division may have a bearing on the mysterious case of Natalie Campbell, whose decomposed remains were unearthed behind an Arlington condominium complex Friday. Police chief Garrett Carter would not comment, but a copy of the report released this afternoon shows Mrs. Angela Campbell, then Angela Mercer, was once reported to the agency on suspicions of child abuse and endangerment."

A fuzzy reproduction of the report appeared on the screen, with Angela's name and the nature of the complaint highlighted.

"No charges were ever filed in the case, which revolved around the testimony of a neighbor who called police in March 1968. The neighbor, who is not identified in the report, claimed to have witnessed Mrs. Mercer shoving the young girl into a car and hitting her several times on the face and arms. Police called to investigate reported seeing no bruises or cuts on the girl and didn't pursue the case.

"This afternoon, investigators looking into the child's murder questioned Mrs. Campbell for nearly forty minutes here in her stately home just off Blue Falls Drive. Neither she nor her husband, attorney Robert Campbell, would comment, except to say the charges were completely unfounded and are in no way connected to Natalie's subsequent disappearance and murder."

The reporter signed off and Carly turned to me. She wiped a tear from my cheek.

"What is it, Em? Did you know Natalie was being abused?"

I shook my head, "No, Joyce did. Or at least she suspected it. But she said Natalie wouldn't talk to her, so she couldn't do anything to help."

"God, that's so awful. I know back then you practically had to have a dozen eye-witnesses to get the police to even look into domestic cases. Forget about proving anything. Wife beaters, child abusers, they could do whatever they wanted. Nobody was there to stop them."

She stood and went into the kitchen, returning with a glass of water and handing it to me.

"God, I can't believe it." I held the cool glass up to my hot face. "Angela was such a wonderful mother, Carly, she loved Natalie so much. I used to always wish my mother was more like her."

"That's the thing about child abuse. You can never tell who's doing it. They can seem like perfect parents, but behind closed doors they take all their shit out on their kids. And the kids keep trying to please them, but it doesn't matter. Half the time they grow up to become child abusers themselves. It's like they don't know any other way."

We sat watching images of Perfect People flicker across the television screen. Suddenly, I thought about the memorial service.

"Oh, my God, Carly. The memorial service— it's tomorrow. What am I going to do? What am I going to say to her?"

"I don't know. Don't say anything. She may be behind bars by then anyway. You don't have to go, you know."

I tried to think. What if Angela hadn't abused Natalie? I'd known her so long, I just couldn't imagine her beating her daughter. Maybe I just wanted to believe it wasn't true. I couldn't bear the thought of Angela beating Natalie to death and then taking her body to the terrace and burying it.

"No, I have to go. What if she didn't do it? I mean, it's only one report. She's suffering enough as it is, I can't just abandon her because of something that may or may not have happened twenty years ago."

"Emma! She may have murdered your best friend! Her own daughter— Jesus Christ."

"I saw her yesterday, Carly. She doesn't look like a murderer or an abuser. She looks lost— so alone."

"Emma, this is not your responsibility. Angela can take care of herself."

"I don't know, she's not that strong. Even when he was ruining her life, it took everything she had to leave Frank. When I was at their house yesterday, I felt like I was intruding, but then Robert left the room and it was strange, I got the feeling Angela wanted to talk to me about something. But she couldn't."

"Probably knew she was going to get caught."

"I can't believe that. I can't believe she beat Natalie. I would have known—I just would have because we were always together. I would have seen something."

"Not necessarily, Em. I worked with abused kids one summer at college. You'd be amazed how parents can hide what they're doing. They claim they aren't in control, but they always manage to leave the scars where no one can see them. Mostly inside."

Another image of Kathy's burned shoulder pushed its way through my mind. I felt the pain she must have felt back then. And yet I could remember her laughing, playing, just like any normal kid. Just like Natalie.

"Well, I have to go to the memorial. Maybe I can try to get her side of the story."

Carly shook her head in resignation. "Don't say I didn't warn you. She's probably going to try to get you to testify in her behalf."

We packed the envelopes back into their boxes and Carly got up to leave. At the door, she put the boxes down and gave me a hug.

"Take it easy, Em. The police will figure it out. Why don't you come have lunch with me tomorrow? Pat and I are meeting at Cymbidium at 1:00." Carly laughed, "Maybe you can grill her for information, too."

Chapter 11

"Brown and Phillips—talk fast, I'm busy."

"Hi, Merry. It's Emma."

"Well, good morning, sunshine. Put it on the chair and shut the door, Ted. I'm not ready for you yet. What's up?"

It took me two months to get used to Meredith Price-Jackson's tendency to talk to seven people at once. I pictured Ted Elliott, her beleaguered assistant, slinking out of her office and rolling his eyes for the billionth time

"I just wanted to let you know I need today off to go to a memorial service."

"The kid in the papers?"

"How did you know?"

"I'm a high-powered executive charged with overseeing four monthly magazines and a weekly newsletter. I know everything. I mean it, Ted, I don't want to see your shining face until I've finished my coffee. Put him on hold. So you knew the girl back in elementary school?"

"Yes, we were...pretty close."

"I'm sorry, kid. Jesus H. Christ, I ask for a simple interview and I get a fucking eulogy. TED! Where the hell have you been? This so-called piece of professional journalism Bryson put together makes the Commissioner sound like a goddamn saint. Get him on the phone and get me some more coffee. Where were we?"

"The memorial service."

"Yeah, right. So is one day enough? You sound like my dish-washer just before it died."

"Actually, I was thinking about taking tomorrow, too. The bluelines on the July issue shouldn't come in till Wednesday—I'll be back by then. I think everything else can wait."

"Well, keep trying." She was talking to Ted again. "And fire the idiot who laid out the August calendar, it looks like my dog did it. Go ahead, babe, I'll take care of things around here. And take it easy, you're the only competent person around here."

"Except you."

"Except me. Call me if you need anything."

I hung up, touched by Merry's concern. 'Call me' is as close as Merry gets to gushing, but with her it means something.

Frowning, I took one last look in the mirror. Dressed in black from head to toe, my skin looked sickly white. I'd put on panty-hose for the occasion and they were already driving me crazy. My stomach was in knots. All I could think about was Angela staring heartbroken out the window. What was I going to say to her?

* * * * *

Mom and I sat on lawn chairs sipping coffee and gazing out over her garden. A misty sunlight fell through the slats in the patio cover, painting stripes of white across my black skirt and shiny calves. Mom was still in her bathrobe, sitting back in the chair with her legs crossed. Her slippered foot bounced to a silent beat.

I watched her as she held her coffee cup in both hands close to her chin, breathing in the rich aroma. We had spoken little since I arrived, both preoccupied with memories, I suppose. I couldn't help comparing today to the rainy morning thirteen years ago when we had buried my grandfather at Arlington Cemetery.

A sparrow flew over the patio cover, casting a fleeting shadow across Mom's face, and landed on the lawn near a cluster of daffodils. It hopped toward us, tossing its glossy head around in search of food.

"I suppose I should get ready," Mom uncrossed her legs and leaned forward, taking another sip of coffee. She smiled as the bird poked its beak into the earth, cocked its head up at her, then went back to digging in the thick grass. She stood. "Come talk to me while I get dressed."

We slipped through the door into the air-conditioned house. Already the temperature was rising outside, burning off the morning dew and casting sharp shadows across the lawn. I sat at the foot of Mom's queen-size bed as she turned on the string of round lightbulbs that run along the top of her vanity mirror. She sat down and opened a gold-capped jar, tapping a fingertip into the soupy beige foundation.

I tried to remember how many times I'd sat here, watching my mother put on her makeup, her back to me, our eyes occasionally meeting in the mirror's spotless glass. We'd talked about school and holidays, vacation plans and her trials and tribulations working as an administrator in a small law office. I'd come out to her in this room.

The room had changed over the years. Pink and green, then blue and silver. Now it was a warm coral, the bed covered in a bulky quilted comforter with matching pillow shams. Deep coral drapes hung at the long windows. She had covered the vanity stool in the same material, and now she sat on it, her back arched, her feet curled underneath the curving wooden feet.

"What are you thinking about, honey?" Her eyes focused momentarily on mine in the mirror and I smiled, shrugging.

"Just remembering how many times we've sat here like this." I leaned on one arm, absentmindedly plucking at the fabric of the comforter.

"Don't wrinkle your blouse, sweetheart, we have to go soon." She closed an eye and began spreading brown eyeshadow across the lid with a spongy applicator.

"You think there'll be reporters there?" I watched as she blended the shadow skillfully up to the brow.

"Oh, I'm sure there will be. It's a shame, though, all that family needs is more people intruding on their privacy." She turned her head back and forth, unconsciously sucking in her cheeks and checking that she'd applied the shadow evenly.

"Did you see the news last night? About Angela being a child abuser?"

"Oh, that's the most ridiculous thing." Mom snapped open a compact and pulled a long-handled sable brush from a porcelain cup by the mirror. "I remember when that happened and it was nothing. Angela was taking Natalie to her father's house, and Natalie didn't want to go for some reason. She had to force the girl into the car. But I'm sure Angela didn't hit Natalie hard, she was just upset. It was only a few months after she left that bastard Frank. She didn't want to see him, naturally, but he'd crashed his car up again—driving drunk, I'm sure—and he insisted Natalie come to his apartment. He had full visitation rights, God knows why, and he threatened to make trouble in court again if Angela didn't comply with the judge's order."

Mom angrily swept blush across her cheeks and forehead, flicking her wrist rapidly and blinking the particles out of her eyes.

"Anyway, someone saw her. I don't know who, they wouldn't tell her. But whoever it was called the cops and when Angela got back they were waiting for her. Of course Natalie was with her father, so they put Angela in a squad car, of all the asinine things, and made her take them to see the child. When they saw Natalie was fine, they dropped the whole thing."

Her arm fell to the table and her eyes glazed over, remembering. "Poor thing, she was so upset. She came over and sat at our dining room table, just crying her eyes out. I felt so sorry for her. I don't think Angela was cut out to be a single mother. And back then the police, the courts, they only listened to men. If a man said he couldn't afford to pay child support they'd say 'Fine, no problem. Just send whatever you can.' Angela was living on a nothing salary and whatever her parents could give her. Frank didn't contribute a dime. I don't know how she managed. And there he was camped in some singles' apartment complex just living it up. I was so happy for her when Robert came along. He's so strong and responsible, never drank.... God knows he's provided for her."

She put away her makeup and got up, walking to the closet and standing in the open door. "I have no idea what to wear. I can't wear the navy suit, they saw you in that Saturday."

"Oh, Mom, they'll never notice." I joined her at the closet, scanning her large wardrobe, most of which was still hanging in plastic dry cleaning bags.

"So tell me about their house. Was it unbelievable?" She took a grey silk blouse and a dark grey suit off the rack and lay them on the bed, bending over to choose a pair of shoes from the plastic stand on the floor.

I picked up the suit and began pulling off the plastic sheath. "It was pretty amazing. It looked like one of those model homes, all black and white and everything matches perfectly. The living room was the size of this house."

"I'll bet. You know, I read in one of my magazines that out in California they're selling houses completely furnished now. Down to the sheets and silverware. I can't imagine letting someone else pick out my sheets. And what do you do with your old stuff? Just throw it away?"

"Well I didn't recognize anything in this place that they had at Oakbrook, that's for sure. Remember how Angela used to have all those old Coca-Cola ads framed on her wall? Now they have paintings of dice and this huge black lamp that curves out behind the couch."

"Probably one of a kind. Lamps are quite the medium for artists now, you know." She wagged a finger at me. "Beautiful *and* functional. I saw a chair downtown designed by some Italian that cost $14,000. Can you imagine spending $14,000 on one chair? What do you do with it?" She struck a Carol Merrell pose beside the vanity chair, a blank grin on her face. "'And this, my friends, is my prize possession, a chair.'"

I laughed. "Angela looks good, though. I think she dyed her hair. It's blonder than I remember it."

"Sweetheart, it's never been blonde. She's always dyed it." Mom took off her bathrobe and hung it on a hanger toward one end of her closet, kicking off her slippers and tucking them into a corner.

"You're kidding? I never knew that. She and Natalie looked so much alike...." I stood at the vanity, tracing a design on one of the cut glass perfume vials clustered to one side.

Mom sat on the bed, gathering up one leg of a pair of panty hose. "Well, I'm sure it was blonde when she was a child.... Shit. Can you hand me that file? This nail keeps catching on my pantyhose."

I pulled an emery board from the porcelain cup and handed it to her, sitting beside her on the bed.

"What about Robert? How did he seem?" The file made a gritty, ripping sound as she drew it along her fingernail.

"He looked tired. I think this is all too much for him. You'd think he'd be used to the spotlight by now, but he was complaining a lot about the reporters."

"I suppose he has a lot on his mind. This is sure to put off his political plans." She hopped to the vanity to put back the emery board, one shrivelled leg of the pantyhose hanging between her legs.

"That's what he said. I feel sorry for him. At least no one's going to fault Angela if she starts crying, but he has to hold it all in. Try to 'be strong.' It's such a crock."

"Well, after they crucified that poor Schneider woman for crying when she quit running for president, I suppose he has to be careful." She stood up, wriggling her hips into the pantyhose.

"Schroeder, Mom, Pat Schroeder. And that was bullshit, too. It's only human to cry. I practically wanted to slap them both Saturday, sitting in that antiseptic room pretending they weren't upset. It isn't good for you." I plucked a bit of fuzz off my skirt, noticing it wasn't as clean as I had thought it was.

"Everyone handles things differently. Maybe it's easier for them this way." She pulled a bra from her dresser and held it to the light. "I need new bras. This thing's falling apart. You want to go shopping next Saturday?" She wrapped the bra around her waist and hooked it in front, twisting it so the closure lay flat against her back.

I reached over and tucked in the faded tag. "Sure."

She looked at me, concerned. "What is it, honey? We don't have to go shopping if you don't want to."

"No, no. That isn't it. I was just thinking about Robert. He said Frank had been by the house. He was pretty upset."

"You're kidding. I suppose he'll be there today, too. Poor Angela, she'll never be totally rid of that bum."

Mom finished dressing and we went into the kitchen. She rinsed our coffee cups and put them in the dishwasher, adding detergent and turning the knob. Running a dishtowel over the counter, she looked around one last time to make sure she hadn't left any dust particles to reproduce in her absence.

We had agreed to take Mom's car to the memorial service, mostly because she didn't want to risk ruining her clothes in the Celica. As we climbed in, she reached over and took my hand.

"I know this is hard for you, sweetie. We don't have to stay for the whole thing. Just let me know when you want to leave."

I gave her hand a squeeze and nodded, a nervous lump forming in my stomach. She backed the car slowly out of the drive and we headed for the church.

* * * * *

The heavy carved doors to the church were propped open; I didn't recognize anyone standing outside, although a few of the faces looked familiar. Mom pointed out Senator Randolph peering out over a group of waxen-faced men on the steps. A group of reporters mingled off to one side, some chatting and laughing too loudly. My mother gave them a searing look as we passed.

We mounted the steps and crossed through the massive doorway into a vestibule that ran the full width of the church. A plaque on the wall proclaimed St. Anthony's one of the oldest Protestant churches in Northern Virginia, erected in 1728 and renovated in 1974. Pews lined the outer wall, and several older women in beaded jackets and hats sat fanning themselves, conferring quietly and glancing up as we walked in. I smiled to them and led my mother through a second set of doors, accepting an engraved program from one of two bored teenage boys in white robes who flanked the entry.

The church itself was large and elegant, with arching stained glass windows running down either side and a huge window portraying Christ on the cross rising above the wide altar. Banks of lilies lined the altar and rose from tall brass sconces set at intervals down the main aisle. Potted plants converged in a leafy mass beside an organ with gleaming brass pipes. Along the side walls, tiers of lit candles flickered, their red glass bowls glowing and fading.

A few people were scattered among the pews, some praying, heads bowed, some reading the program or admiring the decorations. A few of the men glanced at their watches and drummed their fingers on the backs of the pews. We sat toward the back, moving to the center of the pew to leave room for latecomers. Mom folded her hands in her lap, looking uncomfortable and chewing the inside of her lower lip.

"It just seems a little strange to me, having a memorial service when the kid's been dead for seventeen years." I turned to see an elderly man and woman settling themselves into the pew behind us. The man was speaking.

"Hush, Albert, for goodness sakes, someone will hear you." The woman sat heavily onto the seat and set her gloved hands on a boxy black patent leather purse in her lap.

"And I don't understand why, no matter how many times I tell you, Nessie, you always have to starch my shirts to within an inch of their life. I'm choking to death here." He pulled at his collar, straining his fleshy neck and butting her chin with an outstretched elbow.

"Albert! Put your arm down. And I didn't starch your shirt, if you must know, it's just gotten too small. I told you months ago you needed to buy some new ones...." She patted her hand on his arm. "My, isn't the altar pretty. Much nicer than those terrible flowers Amos ordered for poor Clara's funeral. I tell you, Albert, when I go, I expect lilies at the very least. Don't you go skimping on me at my own funeral."

Albert muttered discontentedly, loosened his tie and folded his arms over his protruding belly.

Mom's expression had softened listening to Nessie and Albert argue. I held Mom's hand and touched my head to hers, opening the program so we could both read. A passage from the New Testament was printed in gold script on the outside, along with the date and time of Natalie's memorial. Inside, the program showed the service was going to be brief, with just three hymns and a eulogy by Reverend James McDonough. A separate printed message from the Campbells indicated they were accepting donations in Natalie's name to be given to Children's Hospital. Guests were invited to attend a short reception at their home following the service.

I folded the program and slipped it inside Mom's purse, looking up as more people entered the church and began taking their seats.

The church was filling up. I recognized several state and national politicians among the congregation. Members of the press, including a man carrying a cumbersome television camera and two others burdened down with lighting equipment, filed in noisily and stood along the back wall. When the last of the guests had settled in, Wilson Bennett strode through the entry, looking around the room and nodding approvingly to himself. He caught sight of the TV camera and frowned deeply, straightening his tie and drawing himself up to his full height, which I knew was no more than 5'4". He walked over and murmured to the burly black man carrying the camera, who had to bend over considerably to hear Bennett. For a second, I feared the camera was going to fall off his shoulder and land on Bennett's head, but the cameraman had a firm grip on it, his muscular arm bulging out from a white t-shirt with the words "Drug-Free Zone" printed on it. He nodded and signalled to two other men to take the lighting equipment outside, briefly speaking with Kevin Johnson, the local reporter covering Natalie's murder investigation. Bennett tugged at his lapels and followed the cameraman through the doorway, avoiding Johnson's amused gaze as he passed.

The outer doors closed, cutting off the light from outside, and the organist began playing a melodic requiem from memory. It sounded familiar. Mom gripped my hand harder.

Robert and Angela entered through the doorway, followed by Lillian and Bobbie. They walked the length of the aisle and Robert paused to usher his daughter and mother into their seats at the front of the chapel. Angela sat without looking at anyone and Robert lowered himself into the pew beside her, resting an arm behind her shoulders. A man in white robes wearing a purple sash entered through a hidden door, nodding to the Campbells and taking his place at the lectern. The organist wound down, holding his final note a full five seconds before stopping and turning to Reverend McDonough.

The minister looked out over the crowd. "What can be said to comfort us as we mourn the death of a child? What words can begin to ease the pain we feel at a life extinguished before it had barely begun? What vengeful God allows a human hand to stop the beating heart of an eight-year-old girl? And what cruel fate leaves us here to bury her, to remember a sorrow we'd sustained so long ago, only to have it rekindled and set aflame again to burn unchecked in our souls?"

I stopped listening to him. Aside from his melodramatic choice of words, the questions he asked couldn't be answered with empty verses from the Bible. There was no answer to the pain I felt sitting there, my mother clutching my hand, a tear creeping down her cheek. The words seemed so hollow, the assurances so insincere. When we stood and sang hymns that promised of a better world to come, a world where children would roam free at the foot of their God, blessed with His divine grace and sheltered in His glorious presence, my heart screamed out. What good had these promises of eternal life been for Natalie? What good were they for me?

Thirty minutes later, we bowed our heads in benediction. The doors opened again, bathing the vestibule in bright sunlight and people began filing out.

Mom and I walked down the steps and stood off to one side, watching as the Campbells accepted the handshakes and embraces of their guests. Angela's powdered face was streaked with tears. Lillian, looking perfectly in control, stood between Robert and Bobbie, who both towered over her. She smiled and nodded at the mourners proffering sympathies, taking each presented hand in both of hers.

Bobbie, on the other hand, looked extremely uncomfortable, restless and squinting against the sun's relentless rays. Occasionally she'd bend her ankle, putting her weight on the outside of her foot and jutting a hip outward. Lillian would then touch Bobbie's arm without looking at her, and Bobbie would straighten up and smile weakly at whomever was passing in front of her.

When most of Robert's business associates had filed through and moved off to their waiting cars, Mom and I approached and got in line. Angela looked up and saw us, smiling through red-rimmed eyes and reaching out to hug my mother warmly when we got to her.

"Oh, Angela, I'm so sorry." My mother blew a kiss past Angela's ear and brushed a stray blonde hair into place. They stood with their hands interlocked.

"Thank you, Ellen, and thank you for coming. I've missed you so much." She embraced Mom again, holding onto her and closing her eyes. "It's so good to see Emma again." She released Mom and took my hand. "Your daughter is so lovely, Ellen. So beautiful...."

Beside her, Robert placed a hand on his wife's shoulder, a warm smile on his face. He drew Lillian and Bobbie toward us.

In the bright sunlight, I could see golden specks glittering in Bobbie's eyes. Freckles dotted the bridge of her nose and her full, wide mouth opened across straight white teeth. She looked into my eyes and took my hand as she had before, brushing her fingertips against my palm. I felt it all the way up my arm.

Suddenly, Angela gasped and drew her handkerchief to her lips. I looked up to see Frank Mercer walking swiftly down the steps of the church, his mud-brown polyester jacket open and his tie hanging at a crooked angle. I couldn't remember seeing him during the service. He looked flushed, his thin hair combed over his scalp and his pants wrinkled at the knee where they'd been folded over a hangar. Mom stepped closer to me, slipping her hand protectively through my arm.

"Listen to me, Angela. We've got to talk. I keep calling you but this pip-squeak yes-man keeps telling me you're 'indisposed.'" He threw an angry glare at Bennett, who had materialized behind Robert.

Robert stepped in front of his wife, gripping Frank's arm roughly. "Listen to *me*, Mercer. No one wants you here. I don't want you coming near my family, do you understand? Bennett is under strict orders not to take your calls, and if I have to, I'll get a restraining order to keep you away from my house *and* my wife. Now turn around and leave before I have you dragged off the grounds."

Frank clawed out of Robert's grip and stepped back, pulling at his tie and running two rough hands down his lapels. Over his shoulder, I could see Kevin Johnson, the reporter, standing beside a cameraman, watching the scene. A tiny red light blinked on and off near the camera's lens.

"Listen yourself, Campbell. I'll talk to whoever I want to talk to and right now I want to talk to Angela. You're not so almighty connected I couldn't take you down if I wanted—"

Robert moved toward Frank, his jaw clenched. A vein pulsated in his throat. "Goddammit, Mercer, I've had all I can stand of your threats. The police are on to you. You're not going to make a buck off your own daughter's death, not if I have anything to do with it. Especially since you killed her."

At this accusation, the reporters rushed forward in a wave of microphones and lenses. Frank panicked, pushing at the reporters and trying to break free of the crowd.

"Mr. Campbell, Mr. Campbell! Is it true the police suspect Mercer of kidnapping Natalie?"

"Do you have any comment, Mr. Mercer?"

"Is it true you're undergoing treatment for drug abuse, Mr. Mercer?" The reporters' feverish cacophony of questions and allegations turned into a barrage.

Finally Robert Campbell called for attention.

"Please, please! Ladies and gentlemen." He took a deep breath. "Please, forgive me for losing my temper. This has been a difficult day for my family. I'm sure you understand emotions run high at a time like this."

Kevin Johnson shouted out, "You've just accused Frank Mercer of killing his own daughter. Are you saying now you didn't mean it?"

Robert faced the reporter squarely. "No, sir, I'm not. I have reason to believe Mr. Mercer may be connected to Natalie's disappearance, and have informed the authorities accordingly."

Flashbulbs went off in all directions.

Robert motioned to Bennett as a black limo pulled up. "I'm sure Chief Carter will be able to update you on the progress of the investigation. I apologize again for the disruption." The family moved quickly to the car. The reporters seized upon Frank.

"How do you respond to Mr. Campbell's accusation?"

"It's bullshit. It's all bullshit. That's all I'm gonna say." Frank wormed away from the crowd and yanked open the door of a red sedan. The tires squealed as he pulled out into the street. Suddenly, all was quiet.

Mom and I walked to the car, still dazed by what we'd just witnessed. I opened the door and glanced over the roof of the car in time to see a blue convertible exit the church parking lot.

The driver was Joyce Slocombe.

* * * * *

We pulled up in front of the Campbells' house twenty minutes later. Mom fixed her makeup in the rear-view mirror, chattering about the size of the house and estimating its worth. I was glad to see her back to normal. She hadn't mentioned the service, or the way she had nearly crushed my fingers during the eulogy. I expected she had been overcome with memories of her father, but I didn't ask.

The living room looked exactly as it had two days ago, but now it was full of people holding glasses and balancing hors d'oeuvres on tiny plates. Senator Randolph commanded the attention of a large group near the fireplace. He was talking animatedly, his hands coming together and sweeping apart in wide gestures of appeal. Occasionally his audience smiled and even laughed in appreciation. I turned to see a look of cold fury locked on my mother's face. I nudged her forward and we continued through the hall past a closed set of double doors and into another room I guessed they would call the drawing room.

A long table covered in a white cloth with black trim was set against one wall. Uniformed waiters served food from domed chafing dishes, and at the far end a bartender poured Bloody Marys into row after row of crystal glasses. I didn't see Robert or Angela anywhere, but Lillian held court over a small group of women from a high-backed wing chair near the door. When she saw us, she left the chair and assumed her role as hostess.

"Mrs. Kendrick, Emma, so good of you to come. Please, help yourselves to hors d'oeuvres and drinks. I was just on my way to the living room." She gave Mom's hands a squeeze and slipped

93

past us, greeting an elderly couple in the foyer.

Mom and I took glasses of seltzer water and stood against the wall, watching the cocktail party progress.

"Ellen! Ellen Kendrick, how are you?" A forty-ish woman wearing a sleek veiled cap over shocking red hair rushed forward, pressing her cheek to Mom's and then holding her at arms' distance. "My God, you look fabulous! How long has it been, seven years...?"

"Yes, Libby, hello. Emma, this is Libby Gaines, we used to work together." Mom smiled her 'Help me, please, I can't stand this person' smile and gently lifted Libby's hands off her shoulders.

"That's Libby Gaines *Sheridan*, now. I finally got him to leave that horse of a wife of his. Come into the living room, Ellen, there's a few people I want you to meet." She led Mom off, trading in her empty glass for another Bloody Mary on the way.

I shrugged helplessly in response to Mom's silent, desperate appeal.

Feeling like a target standing alone by the wall, I walked out the door and into the empty foyer. I could hear lively conversation coming from the living room, punctuated by sporadic applause. An icy chill ran down my spine and my mouth grew dry listening to it. My eyes burned with unshed tears. I ducked through the double doors and shut them behind me, leaning against the cool wood.

I'd found my refuge in Robert's den—that dark masculine room where I'd imagined him drinking away his sorrows. Just as I had pictured, the walls were lined with built-in bookcases, two brown wing chairs with matching footstools set at an angle before the fireplace. In one corner, a wide mahogany desk faced into the room, a green banker's lamp centered on the polished surface. The drapes were open, but embroidered sheers suffused the sunlight so that the far corners of the room were steeped in shadow.

I walked toward the fireplace and sat in one of the wing

chairs, pulling a packet of Kleenex from my purse. Chilly air flowed through a vent in the ceiling, hitting my feet as they rested on the footstool. I pulled them up underneath me, turning sideways in the chair and studying a painting on the wall beside the fireplace—some naval battle I recognized but couldn't remember. I squinted, trying to read a small brass plaque set in the frame, and made out the word "Merrimack." It was a Civil War battle, the first between two ironclad ships, but the other ship's name wouldn't come to me.

I was going through the alphabet, sounding out possibilities when the door opened and I heard Lillian's voice.

"I understand that, Senator, but you must understand *my* position. Robert's career is at a crucial point, and I don't believe it serves anyone to put it on hold while this investigation runs its course." She sounded polite but urgent.

"Lillian, darling, I know exactly how you feel, but there's only so much I can do."

"Gene, the answer is as plain as the rather considerable balance in your checkbook. Frank Mercer killed that child. I fail to understand why it is taking so long for an indictment?"

Senator Randolph coughed. "I can try to persuade the District Attorney to get a move on, but you must have more patience, my dear. There is the matter of evidence, and so far they have nothing solid linking Mercer to the girl."

"Don't patronize me, Gene. We both know these things can be arranged. At least have Mercer brought in for questioning. The sooner this matter is cleared up, the sooner Robert can proceed with his announcement."

The Senator sighed in resignation. "Of course, Lillian. I'll do what I can."

When they left, I realized I'd been completely out of sight curled up in Robert's big chair. I'd also been holding my breath.

I felt somewhat guilty about eavesdropping, even involuntarily, but their comments did shed light on Lillian Campbell's priorities. Natalie's murder meant nothing more to her than a delay in her son's political career.

I got up and wandered over to the window. Parting the sheers, I looked out over a wide expanse of lawn that sloped down toward a thick mass of birch trees bordering the property. In my mind, I went over the scene in front of the church.

Clearly, the Campbells knew more about Frank Mercer than had been reported in the press. What if they were right, if Frank *had* killed Natalie? He was many things—an alcoholic, chronically unemployed—but it was hard to believe he was a murderer. I kept seeing him standing in the shadows of our townhouse at Oakbrook, looking up into his daughter's window. Had he been plotting her kidnapping even then? Frank seemed the only likely suspect, but it didn't make sense for Lillian to rush the investigation. The longer it drew out, the more Robert could display his chiselled features on the evening news. I wondered if Lillian was powerful enough to force an arrest. I knew she was well connected in the legal community, her late husband had been a judge and her father had served as Virginia's Attorney General in the 1950s.

The windows in the den faced west, in the direction of National Airport. I watched as a silver jet floated silently toward the earth, disappearing behind the trees. My eyes followed the plane's trajectory to the ground and in the shadow of the trees about five-hundred feet from the house, I saw two people arguing.

Bobbie still wore her black dress, but now she held her shoes in one hand. The black heels crashed together as she threw her arms around, yelling at someone standing beneath the trees. I strained to see who it was, but couldn't. Abruptly, Bobbie marched toward the house, looking directly up at the den, and me. Even from five hundred feet, her eyes made my knees weak. I ducked behind the sheers, flattening myself against the wall.

When my heart stopped pounding, I slumped against the wall, convinced I was going out of my mind. Why was I hiding from Bobbie? Why did she scare me so much? I was taking all of this too seriously, trying to decipher people's motives and spying on Natalie's family. I envisioned Mrs. Huntemann amid her crewelwork pillows, her eyes sparkling with excitement. How had I let her convince me to find out who killed Natalie? How had I allowed myself to reach the point where I was plastered against the wall in the Campbells' den?

I took a deep breath, noticing the room seemed brighter than it had moments before. Or maybe reality was just breaking through. Finally. I set my purse on Robert's desk and tucked in my blouse, wishing there was a mirror in the room. As I reached for my purse, I happened to glance at Robert's appointment book. For the next week, seven dated columns ran down the page. He'd listed several appointments under each date. One name caught my eye. On Tuesday at 4:30 p.m., Robert had written "J. Slocombe."

I flipped back a few pages, and Joyce's name appeared two other times over the past few weeks. I couldn't figure it out. Was Robert seeing Joyce professionally? And if he was, why had she pretended not to know him when I talked to her?

Chapter 12

Natalie and I were kneeling at the top of the stairs, peeking through the wooden banister. Down in the living room, Angela and Robert were playing with Bobbie on the floor. Lillian sat in a chair, her arms out to the baby. Bobbie giggled with delight as she toddled from her mother to her father to her grandmother across the shag carpet.

"That's my girl! She can crawl up the stairs now, too, Mother. Go to Grandma, Bobbie, there you go."

Lillian combed her fingers through the little girl's dark hair. "Oh, Robert, must you call her 'Bobbie'? It sounds so common."

"Mother, she's just a child. Besides, she looks like a Bobbie to me." Robert held Angela's hand in his lap.

"She'll grow into her name, Lillian. It just doesn't seem right calling a baby 'Barbara.'" Angela scooted closer to her husband.

"The name was fine for *my* mother."

Lillian sat Bobbie formally on her lap. Natalie and I watched as Bobbie quickly scooted away and grabbed a camera from a nearby end table. She picked it up in both hands and stuck her face in the lens, grinning. Robert and Angela laughed as Lillian extricated the camera from Bobbie's powerful grip.

"Now Barbara, the first thing you must learn is poise. Just stand still and smile." Lillian focused the camera, but just as she was ready to press the shutter release, Bobbie sat down with a thump and pulled her skirt over her head. More laughter floated up from the room.

"I can see I have a lot to teach you, young lady. Here, now, go to your Daddy, I want to take a picture of the three of you."

Lillian stood and focused the camera on her son and daughter-in-law. Bobbie waddled over and Robert picked her up, setting her on his lap and arranging her pale blue dress around her plump legs. Angela squeezed his arm.

"Oh, Robert, you have a such a lovely family. I do wish your father could have seen this." Lillian snapped the picture.

Beside me, Natalie rose silently and turned away, walking into her room and closing the door.

Chapter 13

A cool blast of sweet, fragrant air greeted me as I pushed through the glass door into Cymbidium. The small dining room smelled of basil and melon, and clear sunlight bounced off the checkerboard tiles in the entry. I began to relax immediately, and met the hostess' smile easily.

"One for lunch?" She wore faded jeans and a lime green t-shirt emblazoned with the cafe's delicate lavender orchid logo.

"Actually, I'm meeting two people. I don't see them, though."

"We have another dining room upstairs. Can I ask who you're meeting?"

I smiled to myself. Only in Cymbidium would the hostess know diners by name.

"Carly Velasquez and Patrice Carroll."

"Like I said, upstairs. Follow me."

She led me through a cluster of small, wrought-iron tables toward a short staircase. I glanced around, taking silent, personal pleasure in the sight of lovers sitting across from each other, fingers interlaced, eyes locked. Peaceful, lilting music filtered through hidden speakers, and those women who weren't deep in conversation ate heartily of the vegetarian fare. I was getting hungrier by the minute passing plates heaped with pasta and lush garden salads.

The cafe was nearly full. Cymbidium, which occupies a renovated storefront in Old Town Alexandria, is the thriving brainchild of two women, Alice Gerard and Julia McClintock. Lovers since high school, they have lived together in Northern Virginia all their adult lives. Alice was formerly the Creative Director at an advertising agency, while Julia worked in the kitchen of a Washington hotel. After saving up for twenty years, they decided to open a women's cafe. Not a bar, but a uniquely quiet, loving haven run by women for women.

I followed the hostess up the short, curving staircase, still trying to decide between the primavera and the fettucini.

"I don't think I've seen you here before. What's your name?" She turned at the top of the stairs, making way for me and indicating Carly and Patrice at a table near the window.

"Emma Kendrick. No, I haven't been here in awhile."

"Well, hope we see you in again soon. I'm Sherry. If there's anything I can do, just whistle."

I headed for the table, noticing that Carly and Pat were both talking at the same time.

"You're absolutely right! There isn't any reason at all!" Carly shook her hair wildly, reaching for a glass of water.

"Well, according to the Powers That Be, homosexuals destroy morale and endanger military secrets—because of our inherent promiscuity and lack of moral standards." Patrice's monologue dripped sarcasm.

"Hey. Hope I'm not interrupting." I took a seat beside Carly.

She gave me a smile. "We were just discussing the government's asshole policy of banning gays from military service. Pat's trying to help those women that got kicked out of Quantico."

Patrice winked at me across the table. "Your misguided friend here seems to think we godless homosexuals have something to contribute in the defense of Freedom."

I edged away from Carly, playing along with Patrice. "You're sick."

"Yeah, I know. We should all be shipped off to some godforsaken island and cut off from decent society. Just think; in forty or fifty years, there'd be none of us left. No one back here to recruit the innocent children of God-fearing Christians."

"Absolutely," Patrice said. "I remember the day I was recruited. Her name was Keesha. She was nineteen years old, with hands like a Rodin sculpture. She gave me a Temporary Membership Card, a complimentary ball-point pen and one of the most exhausting—and thrilling—nights of my life."

"You only got a ball-point pen? What a gyp! I got a toaster-oven."

I enjoyed making Patrice Carroll laugh. Her eyes sparkled merrily, turning a haunting gold to augment the warm honey-brown of her skin. Her black hair was thickly braided and gathered in a multi-colored scarf. She wore a silky fuschia tank top and had another scarf wound around her waist. Beaded earrings cascaded from her ears, sketching invisible lines on her bare shoulders.

"Carly, darling, perhaps you'd care to properly introduce this delightful woman."

"Whoops! Major etiquette *faux-pas* on my part. Patrice Carroll, Emma Kendrick."

We shook hands over the table, her grip warm and strong. She stared into my eyes as if she knew something I didn't, and found it amusing.

"Emma, lovely name. Carly tells me you work for *Perspective.*"

"I'm the Assistant Editor, but I pretty much do everything. Except write the articles."

"I read it often. Fascinating. The interview with Faye Wattleton last April was surprisingly revealing."

"I thought so too. She's a wonderful woman."

"Wonderful." She rolled the word over her tongue. "Yes, I suppose she is."

Patrice was mocking me. I wanted to say something intelligent. Something filled with meaning and insight. But all I could think of was how unbelievably attractive Pat looked in fuchsia.

"How was the memorial service?" Carly asked.

I'd almost forgotten Carly was sitting beside me.

"Oh, okay, I guess. There was a scene afterwards, though. Natalie's natural father showed up and got into this huge argument with Robert. I'm sure it'll be on the news. He accused Frank of kidnapping Natalie and killing her."

"Jesus. You think he did it?" Carly seemed thrilled by the news.

"I guess it's possible. Mrs. Huntemann said he used to hang around Oakbrook and watch the house. She said he was there that night."

"So Dorothy Huntemann is still haunting this Earth?" Patrice lit a long brown cigarette and exhaled a stream of blue smoke toward the ceiling.

"Her soul must be a thousand years old. I have always felt fortunate to have known her."

Patrice licked her lower lip unconsciously. Something inside me melted. Patrice smiled and tapped her cigarette against the ashtray. "How's your job search progressing, Carly?"

"Slowly. I applied to that think-tank in San Francisco I told you about. They're supposed to call by Friday for an interview."

My stomach did a somersault. Carly hadn't told me she'd applied for the job, just that she'd heard about it.

"I do envy you." Pat stubbed out her cigarette and pushed the ashtray toward the window. "San Francisco. When you get out there, you must remember to call me. I know a few women you'll want to connect with—"

Carly whistled suggestively.

"To get *involved*." Patrice raised a reproving eyebrow. "One in particular, Isabelle Stone, can get you in anywhere. Oh, there's so much you can do. I remember when I was younger and staying in a women's commune near the Marina...."

I tuned her out, unable to listen to them any longer. They just assumed Carly would be boarding a plane to California at any moment. It was Judy all over again. I signalled the waitress for more water.

"You ready to order?"   She set the water pitcher pointedly beside me after refilling my glass.

Patrice handed over her menu without looking at it. "The shrimp, I think, Marie. And mineral water. Thank you."

"Carly?"

"Oh, God. I can't decide. You go, Emma."

I studied the menu, a sheet of laminated pink paper covered front and back with handwritten choices. I knew I needed food— I couldn't remember when I had eaten last—but now nothing appealed to me. I read through a list of pastas accompanied by thick herbed sauces and my insides threatened to launch an offensive.

"Um, the Oriental Salad, I guess. And a Diet Pepsi?"

Marie made a face and shook her head in mock scorn.

"Oh, right. I forgot you don't serve soft drinks. I'll just have mineral water."

"Much better. For you *and* the salad. Carly, you know you're going to get the fettucini, so why am I still standing here?"

"All right, all right, But eighty-six the olives this time."

Marie stuck her tongue out at Carly, and Carly responded in kind.

All of a sudden I was overcome with memories of sitting here with Judy, Carly, and Carly's Woman-of-the-Week. We used to come here constantly, bantering and flirting with the waitresses, talking for hours at one of the tiny tables. I hadn't been back since Judy left. I missed it. And now Carly was leaving, too.

"Oh, Pat, I almost forgot. Emma met one of your castaways this weekend. What was her name?"

"Joyce Slocombe." I watched Patrice for her reaction. There was none.

"How is she? I haven't seen her in years."

"She has a private practice in Brookside."

"Quite a coincidence, your running into Joyce. But, if you see her again, give her my best."

Carly followed the conversation like a tennis match, looking from me to Patrice and back again. A puzzled frown pulled her full, black eyebrows closer together.

"Am I missing something here? You women sound like you're talking in code."

Patrice shrugged. "Emma is probably wondering why I should want to give Joyce Slocombe 'my best.' She and I parted on rather disparate terms. I'm sure she relayed that to Emma." Patrice's golden eyes never left me.

I looked up, flames licking at my cheeks. "She didn't go into detail. She just told me you guys broke up."

"You *guys*?" Carly glared at me.

"I'm sure she did." Pat said.

"Pat, tell us everything." Carly plunged her fork into the pasta and shoved a frightening amount of it into her mouth.

Pat smiled but with a tightness, just missing real humor. "She was young, I was young. We fell in love. I was her first—a situation I'm sorry to say I've found myself in all too often—and she was afraid. We argued incessantly about her coming out to her coworkers and her family. Eventually, we grew apart. End of story."

Pat pierced a shrimp on her plate.

"That's it? No shameless pleading? No knock-down drag-out floor fights? No malicious recriminations?"

"No, just a simple parting of the ways. It *does* happen, Carly, dear."

"Yeah, but...." Carly turned to me in appeal. She hates stories that don't involve a certain amount of intrigue.

I decided this was my cue. "Mrs. Huntemann told me you and Joyce had a fight...I mean, she said she thought she heard you arguing the night Natalie Campbell disappeared."

"The night...? Oh yes, I remember that night. Poor Joyce. I suppose I was terribly hard on her. I believe at that point Joyce had finally agreed to tell her coworkers she was a lesbian, but she steadfastly refused to tell her parents. In retrospect, I'm sure I could have benefitted from a little understanding. But I was unflinching in my political activism and thoroughly unwilling to accept partial victory on any front…. I'm afraid I came on a little strong. And Joyce, well, first she tried to sway me, then she tried to meet me halfway…. She even tried the popular 'I don't want to share our love' approach. That was the first time I'd heard it. I nearly fell for it."

Patrice speared another shrimp and chewed it slowly, gazing out the window. In profile, she looked like Cleopatra. She swallowed and licked a finger, addressing the rest of her story to me.

"That particular night, Joyce called her mother from my house. I had given her an ultimatum of sorts. She came very close to telling her family the truth, but in the end she backed down. I got angry, she stormed out. A few hours later, I went looking for her but I couldn't find her. So I went to sleep. The next morning, her car was gone. We made up a few days later, but neither of us forgot the things we'd said. And she never told me where she'd gone that night. Certainly not to her mother's…."

We sat in silence for a few moments, each remembering our own struggle with the Truth. With telling our families and friends. I picked at my salad, picturing Joyce so confident in her apartment and so confused back then. In love and afraid— emotionally torn apart. We'd all been there. Patrice seemed to regret not having given Joyce the support she needed, but at the same time something in her voice suggested she wasn't telling the whole story.

"She sounds like a wimp." Carly snorted. I knew why. Carly has precious little pity for closeted gays. That's near the top of my 'Never-to-be-Mentioned' list.

"Quite the opposite, in fact. Joyce can react like a wounded wildcat if she feels cornered. The things she said to me…. And she wasn't like that only with me, either. I once saw her make confetti out of the school board chairman over the district's program for integrating disabled students. Joyce's younger sister was born mentally retarded, and she held a fierce grudge against anyone who thought the disabled were incapable of learning or participating in society. I did respect her for that. She wouldn't give an inch."

"Oh, big temper, eh?" Carly spoke with her mouth full.

"Yes, and assertive women like Joyce are still perceived as a threat. By their lovers at times, and society at large. But her temper serves it's purpose—for her survival, and in moving others to action." Patrice shrugged, pushing her empty plate forward and lighting another cigarette.

I pondered whether she and Joyce could ever renew their relationship. Now that they were older, more sure of themselves.... That thought, of course, led into a mental fantasy about Judy and I running into each other twenty years down the road. I imagined us bumping into each other at an airport. We'd look into one another's eyes and realize our love had never died. She'd pull me close and kiss my cheek, my eyelids, my lips....

"Emma! I said, what did Joyce tell you about Natalie?"

I came back to Ground Zero to find both Carly and Patrice watching me expectantly.

"She said she thought Natalie had been abused."

"I'm sorry to hear that," Patrice said sympathetically. "Was Joyce able to help?"

"No. She said Natalie wouldn't talk to her about it."

"Not surprising. Abused children often blame themselves. They don't want to cast their parents in a bad light. They're convinced something they're doing is provoking the abuse. If they would just behave, get better grades, clean their rooms, everything would be all right. So tragic."

I folded my napkin beside my nearly untouched salad and sipped the tangy mineral water. It still didn't fit. I knew I was missing something. I tried to focus on Natalie. To remember if she had ever hinted at—

"Oh, my...I've just remembered. You lived at Oakbrook, as well, didn't you?" Patrice eyed me with new interest.

"Yes. I thought you knew that."

107

"No, I hadn't put it together until now. Age, you know. Oh, and I do feel old now. I can see the two of you running past my living room window just as clear...."

I smiled. "Actually, Natalie once saw you and Joyce kissing through your living room window."

Patrice froze for an instant.

"That was Natalie?"

"Yes, she said Joyce went nuts and shut the drapes as fast as she could."

Carly giggled.

Patrice's golden eyes darkened to a flinty brown, then brightened again as if they were controlled by some hidden dimmer switch. "Yes, well, as I said, Joyce wasn't ready to accept her lesbianism. I'm sure we all went through that phase."

"Not me." Carly said, with pride.

"We all can't hope to know ourselves as fully as you do, dear." Patrice was herself again, the shadow gone from her face.

I thought about what Patrice had said—that Joyce reacted violently when she felt cornered.

"Do you think Joyce could have been afraid Natalie would tell someone about the kiss?"

Patrice studied me. She weighed her words carefully. "I suppose each of us has something we hold so precious that we'd do anything to protect it."

Carly's eyes widened. She looked at me, "You don't think Joyce did it, do you?"

I didn't answer. A part of me saw the same strong woman I'd met on Sunday, fighting for her privacy, her fear of exposure. Could she have been that afraid of Natalie?

Patrice broke through my thoughts.

"Perhaps I've painted a distorted picture of Joyce. She was afraid back then, and very protective of her privacy, but more than anything Joyce Slocombe loved children. In fact, I think the prospect of never bearing a child of her own scared her more than society's condemnation of homosexuality. Back then, being gay rather ruled out parenthood.

Tell me, did she ever have children?"

"I don't know. She didn't mention any."

I tried to listen to Patrice's reason. More than anything, I didn't want to believe Joyce was capable of murdering Natalie. I was still hoping she'd call. I wanted to talk to her again. I wanted to trust her.

"Joyce would have been a wonderful mother." Patrice emphasized the word wonderful, a clear reference to my limited descriptive powers.

I smiled, thinking Patrice looked wonderful when she said the word 'wonderful.'

"How is Natalie's mother, Angela? I do wish I could have expressed my sympathies to her." Patrice tilted her head in concern. An earring clicked musically against her throat.

"She's pretty broken up. Actually, she's the one they're accusing of child abuse."

"Angela? Why that's insane." Patrice dismissed the charge easily. "Angela was the sweetest soul. I remember the day I moved in at Oakbrook, she came over and brought me cookies—on one of her own dishes. You can imagine many of the residents weren't happy to see an African-American woman—alone—moving into their white suburban enclave. And dressed in traditional Nigerian costume, as well. But Angela welcomed me with open arms. Such a warm woman. Of course, this was before she remarried. I didn't see her much after that."

"No, I suppose not." My mother had said the same thing more than once. She called it one of the 'side effects' of marriage.

"You people plannin' on leaving, or should I arrange to have your mail forwarded?" Marie materialized beside me, fanning herself comically with her notepad.

"Oh, give it a rest, Scarlett, nobody here gives a damn." Carly's face lit up, though she tried bravely to hide it.

"Why, Rhett, such language—you make a girl blush." Marie dropped the check diplomatically between us and blew Carly a kiss.

We split the bill, leaving Marie a generous tip, and got up to leave. As Carly stopped to plan a date with Marie, Patrice put a hand on my shoulder and leaned over to kiss my cheek.

"I'm very sorry for your loss, Emma. I wish there was something more I could do to help."

I nodded, thinking that if anything, talking to her had left me more confused than ever.

Chapter 14

Lunchtime at Paulsen Elementary. I wandered the halls alone, dodging giggling groups of students who walked toward the cafeteria. Various colorful signs printed on stiff, shiny cardboard adorned the walls of the hallway, reminding me to look before crossing the street and to eat something from each of the four basic food groups every day. I scanned every passing face looking for Natalie.

We always ate lunch together. We'd troop through the cafeteria line lugging our blue plastic trays laden with pizza, macaroni and cheese, whatever the day's entree happened to be. Natalie always drank apple juice, so I did too, even though I thought it made the macaroni taste funny. When the weather was nice, we'd eat outside, sitting on the stone benches that bordered the playground. Otherwise, we ate inside at a table near the back of the cafeteria, where everyone could see that no boys ever sat with us.

Today it was warm and sunny, and I couldn't find Natalie anywhere. I knew that if we didn't get outside soon, we'd have to sit on the ground.

Natalie had been quiet all through math class, answering my notes only with a perfunctory "yeah" or "I know" awkwardly scrawled with her left hand. I thought she was worried about the test Friday, so I wrote that I'd help her study at lunch. But she slipped out of the room just as the bell rang.

I rounded a corner, math book in hand, noticing that the crowd in the halls had nearly disappeared. Through the glass doors to the playground, I could see the benches filling up. I watched as two fifth-graders took our usual spot. Where was Natalie?

Down the hall, Miss Slocombe's office door opened and I saw Natalie come out, juggling her math book and a small white purse. She looked really upset. She paused in the doorway to sling the purse over her shoulder and Miss Slocombe appeared behind her. Miss Slocombe looked even more upset.

Natalie started to walk away, but Miss Slocombe pulled her back. I was scared for Natalie. Whenever a kid had to see Miss Slocombe, it usually meant they were in trouble. But I couldn't think why Natalie would be in trouble. Unconsciously, I stepped closer to the wall and held my breath, watching.

Miss Slocombe knelt on one knee in front of Natalie, resting her hand on Natalie's shoulder. Their faces close together, Miss Slocombe spoke deliberately, slowly, nodding her head. My mother spoke like that when she was really mad. Her voice got low and her hands shook. I imagined Miss Slocombe's hand trembling against Natalie's thin shoulder.

I couldn't hear their exact words; but I saw Natalie stiffen. She backed away, her eyes wide and shining even from where I stood. She screamed "NO!" and ran down the hall away from me.

Miss Slocombe rose to her feet and called after her. "Natalie! Natalie, come back!"

But she had disappeared around the corner by then.

Miss Slocombe wiped a palm across her forehead, closing her hand into a tight fist and hitting her head lightly in frustration. Then she turned and saw me. I took a quick, guilty step backward, pulling my math book closer to my chest. She didn't come after me. Instead, she just went back into her office and closed the door.

I ate lunch alone that day, sitting on the ground against the cool wall of the school, pretending to study long division. Natalie found me just before the bell rang.

"Where were you?" I asked.

"No place. Sorry I didn't have lunch with you."

"I saw you talking to Miss Slocombe."

"Oh." She looked away, shading her eyes with a curved hand.

"Are you in trouble?"

"No."

I waited for her to explain, but she didn't.

Chapter 15

Tuesday—my second day off—I sat cross-legged on the couch and watched Julia Child prepare a steaming rack of lamb in two minutes on *Good Morning America*. I'd been up for over an hour, and so far I'd heard more than I wanted to know (or could even begin to comprehend) about the S&L crisis, an interview with the scruffy star of Hollywood's latest multi-million dollar bloodfest, and three different weather forecasts. I clicked the mute button and flipped open the paper.

I read the first section of the paper, realizing halfway through that it was exactly the same as what I'd heard last night on the eleven o'clock news. I decided to change my subscription so I'd only get the paper on Sunday.

Standing in front of the refrigerator, I warily contemplated a plastic container I couldn't remember putting in there. Fortunately the phone rang, saving me from having to open it.

"Emma, this is Merry. I know you're at home wallowing in grief and I wouldn't be calling you if this wasn't an absolute emergency but we've got a doozy over here."

"Merry, slow down. What's wrong?"

"It appears Hank, our trusty printer, has 'misplaced' two signatures of the July issue. The bluelines came in sixteen pages short. I've got the flats in front of me and...they're not here. Just a second, Emma, I'm putting you on hold."

I held the phone away from my ear, a Toyota commercial blaring through the receiver. I was flattered Merry needed my help to straighten out a problem. Suddenly, I realized I wanted to be at work. I wanted to be busy.

Merry came back on the line. "I hate these phones. I'd fire the idiot who bought them except I think it was me. Hank says he can't find the flats anywhere. Claims they weren't delivered with the rest of the issue."

"That can't be true. I put them together myself."

"Emma Kendrick, are you calling Hank, beloved Hank, Hank who could eat us both bones and all and still have room for half a cheesecake, a *liar*? Shocking. And I was going to put him in my will. Well, just tell me where the files are in case we have to re-paste everything."

"Listen, I'm coming in. We're ahead of schedule this month, so don't start recreating the artwork till I get there. I'm sure if I talk to Hank I can get this straightened out."

"Emma, you're a saint. I'll see you when you get here."

Fifteen minutes later, I was easing the Celica through the congested Washington traffic, the windows down and my hair still wet from the shower. My mind was already working through the problem of the missing magazine pages.

* * * * *

I never planned to go into publishing. When I got out of college, I had no idea what I wanted to do. My degree in management meant precious little to Washington employers, annually besieged with college graduates expecting at the very least vice presidencies and company cars. In desperation, I took a job as a receptionist at Brown & Phillips just to pay the bills. A few months later, I was a secretary in the Entertainment Division, which publishes our tackiest—and, as a result, most profitable—magazines. I met Merry there, over the phone as I intercepted her frequent calls to the Senior Editor, Mr. Harriman. We got along from the start, unlike Mr. Harriman and Merry, who are still mortal enemies. My dear friend Kate, Harriman's personal secretary, used to direct Merry's calls my way so Merry could be 'impressed with my abilities', as Kate so generously put it. Then, one day, Merry called my extension. I was an Assistant Editor in the Women's Division before noon.

It happened so fast, I sometimes think it's all been a dream. I enjoy my work—editing the articles that will appear in *Perspective*, soothing the egos of our free-lance writers and approving the layout of the magazine every month—but sometimes I'm afraid I'm having too much fun. My only other experience with working has been vicariously through my mother, who tolerates her job, but looks to her volunteer work for real fulfillment. I tell myself I'm still getting used to the job and eventually it will get routine and lose its appeal. But for now, as I took the Route 7 exit and planned my strategy to recover the lost pages of *Perspective*, I smiled to myself. My personal life might be on the critical list, but at least I had my work.

The elevator doors opened onto a publisher's battle scene: bustling secretaries, assistants and editors shouting over the noise of desk drawers slamming, copiers copying and phones ringing unanswered. Over all of it, I could hear Merry screaming for her assistant Ted, who was standing at his desk with a phone receiver clamped to each ear.

"Emma, thank God! Ted, Emma's here!" Chris, the Production Manager, waved and went back to sorting through a pile of the cardboard 'flats' that become the pages of *Perspective*.

Ted frantically signalled me to his desk, and put both lines on hold as I dropped my canvas bag on his chair.

"Hank says he's looked everywhere, and the flats just aren't there. Chris is checking through the back files, but I can't imagine they'd be there—any ideas?"

"Let me check the Art Department and a few other places. Don't worry, I've got it all on disks, we can recreate the whole issue if we have to."

I grabbed my bag and turned toward my desk. Ted's left hand, bearing the gold band his life partner, Brian, had given him twelve years ago, clamped down on my shoulder.

"Darling, you're not going *anywhere* till you tame the Wild Thing in there. I tossed in a side of raw beef half an hour ago, but she's still chomping for blood."

I took a deep breath and turned toward Merry's door, on which hangs a stop sign bearing the words, *ASK YOURSELF: IS IT REALLY WORTH IT?*—a present from Ted.

I knocked and walked in, settling myself as best I could in the Hot Seat, a remarkably uncomfortable chair Merry hand-picked to put in front of her desk. She was on the phone, but she managed to communicate anyway. A series of evocative eye movements told me she was glad I was here, she had her period and she was arranging Hank's death to look like an accident.

"I know that, Hank.... Listen—yes, I know, just listen to me. Why don't we try something a little different here. Write this down: Lift your feet off your desk, put down the cigar, heave yourself out of your chair and walk—don't run, we don't want you to risk a stroke—*walk* down to the pressroom and look around yourself.... I realize it's in another building, but then, so is the lunchroom which I believe you've visited once or twice...." Merry stuck a well-chewed fingernail down her throat. "Just do it, Hank. Call me when you're done."

She set the phone ever-so-gently back in the cradle and mimed unloading both barrels of a shotgun into it.

"If he didn't give me free color proofs and a case of Moet every Christmas, I'd yank his balls off myself."

"Don't worry about it. We'll find them."

"Sorry I had to drag you in here. How was the service?"

"It was difficult. Actually, I'm glad to be here. I was going nuts at home."

"Ah, home. I had one of those once. Gave it up for lent. I saw the news. Think Mr. Polyester's our man?"

"Frank Mercer? I don't know. He seems like the most likely candidate, but why would he hang around once they found the body? You'd think he'd head for the hills without looking back."

"Maybe he's after something. Could be the kid's death is just the tip of the iceberg."

I nodded, suspecting she was right.

"Maybe I ought to put Harriman on to this. Might make a good cover story for one of his rags. We need an angle, though... Mercer did look a little like Elvis."

She gave me a heartfelt look that said the things she couldn't say out loud and picked up the phone.

"Enough, you'll get hemorrhoids sitting in that chair. Get to work. Blake's piece on Barbara Bush is one of the missing pages. If she finds out, we're gonna be up to here in shrieking spandex and *Georgio*. Hello, Kate, is he in yet? I'll talk to you later, Em. Take it easy. Too late, love, tell him I already heard his tie...."

* * * * *

"Hey, Em, you ready?' Kate stepped over the flats scattered across the floor and came up behind me at my computer terminal.

"Two seconds, let me print this so I can send it down to paste-up."

"Couldn't find the pages, huh?"

"Nope."

"I'm sorry. I know you wanted to take today off."

Kate's soft voice was suffused with sympathy. It felt like the heat from a fireplace penetrating frostbitten toes. I longed for the warmth, but it meant going through painful pins and needles as the skin came back to life.

"That's okay." I stacked the printed pages and slipped them into an envelope. "It's good to be busy, you know?"

Kate smiled, her almond-shaped eyes crinkling at the corners. Her sandy blonde hair was pushed up under a straw hat wrapped with the same flowered material that made up her loose-fitting jumper. She wore flat canvas shoes and bobbie socks. She looked like an extra from Little House on the Prairie—an image she fosters. Carly calls it Kansas Drag.

"Where to?" I grabbed my canvas bag and fished out my wallet, counting seven dollars and a subway farecard with fifteen cents left on it. "Someplace cheap. I'm tapped out."

"Carolina's?"

"Sure. We can eat outside. I just have to drop this in the Art Department on the way out."

At Kate's invitation, Ted joined us—purposefully not letting Merry know he was leaving. We walked to the nearby restaurant, Kate regaling me with a detailed account of Harriman's latest gambit. In short (excuse the pun), he left a shopping bag full of dirty underwear on Kate's desk and asked her to wash it because his wife was out of town. She took it into the ladies' room, got everything soaking wet, and draped it over the furniture in his office while he was in a meeting. He came back, saw it and mumbled something about holding his calls. For half an hour, the unmistakable whine of a blow dryer emanated from behind his door.

We commandeered a picnic table, unloading white paper bags filled with deli sandwiches and seedless grapes wrapped in wax paper. I sat across from the two of them, noticing once again how much Ted and Kate look alike.

Ted leaned over and whispered something to Kate, who tilted her chin skyward and clapped a hand over her hat. Both blond and tanned, they looked like a print ad for Newport cigarettes.

"What's so funny?" I popped the tab on a Diet Pepsi.

"The guy at the table behind you just picked his nose and ate it."

"Oh, for God's sake, Ted, I'm eating!" But I had to laugh. As most of his friends will tell you, Ted keeps you young. Whether you like it or not.

Kate, still laughing, tossed a grape into the grass. A sparrow hopped up and struggled to spear the fruit with its beak. "So, Em, how's it going? I was surprised when Merry said you were coming today."

"Oh, all right, I guess. I was going to stay home, but I felt really restless. When she called about the missing pages, I figured I might as well come in."

"And miss *Geraldo*? I saw the preview—today's topic was 'Circumcision: Is it ever too late?' I taped it."

"You couldn't afford it, Ted, there'd be nothing left." Kate pelted him with a grape. "Now shut up, we're supposed to be supporting Emma."

Kate turned to me, concern filling her near-violet eyes. "This must be really hard on you."

"Yeah, I guess. It's hard to describe, you know? Sometimes I feel like I've lost the closet friend I ever had, and other times I can't even remember her. It's like there's something my mind's blocking out, something really important. But I try so hard, and I can't figure it out."

"Hey, hey, hey. Don't beat yourself up." Kate closed a warm hand over mine. "You know, you do that a lot."

Ted eyed me suspiciously, tapping the aluminum cap from his Perrier on the wooden table top.

"You're up to something. Spill it."

I hadn't meant to mention my 'detective work,' but Ted could always tell when there was something on my mind. I considered what to tell them. Carly was so opposed to my getting involved in Natalie's murder investigation, I didn't want Kate and Ted telling me I was a fool, too.

"Well, there's this woman, Mrs. Huntemann. She lives at the apartment complex where Natalie and I lived. I went and saw her on Saturday. It's long story, but she sort of made me feel like it was up to me to figure out why Natalie died."

"Maybe she's right." Kate released my hand. "Dr. Clements says sometimes we can't settle for other people's explanations. It's better for us to find our own answers."

"Dr. Clements, Dr. Clements.... The way you talk about her, I'm beginning to think this is more than a professional relationship." Ted was peeling the label off his Perrier bottle.

"You're just jealous because your shrink couldn't do anything more for you." Kate teased.

Ted did his best Anthony Perkins impression. "She's lying. I'm fine, just fine. Mother? Mother, is that you?"

As we laughed, a thought occurred to me.

"Kate, do you think therapy is really helping you?"

"God, yes. Just having someone to talk to really makes it easier. Why? Are you finally going to take my advice?"

"I was thinking about it. I met this woman—she used to be the counselor at my elementary school. She's in private practice now. I talked to her on Sunday and I keep thinking about it...." I trailed off, unable to explain what I was feeling.

"What's stopping you?" Kate's voice held a soft, velvety quality that reminded me of Joyce.

"I don't know. Carly said shrinks are a waste of time and money."

"Carly's more in need of a good therapist than anyone I've ever met, next to Ted."

"Mother? I hear you, Mother!"

Kate dug her elbow into Ted's ribs.

"Really, Em, you can't let Carly influence your decision. If talking to this woman made you feel better, maybe you should go back."

I looked at my sandwich, chicken salad piled high in a buttery croissant. Normally one of my favorites, today it looked ready to eat me. I tore off a piece and dropped it to the ground for the birds to fight over.

"Emma? Talk to me. Is it just Natalie's death that's bothering you?"

I sipped my soda, resigned to the fact that I'd probably never eat again.

"No, actually we talked a lot about Judy."

"Oh." Kate and Ted shared a meaningful glance. Both committed to long-term relationships, they appreciated more than Carly ever could how Judy's leaving had devastated me.

"I'll tell you something, Emma. The thing about therapy is that it focuses entirely on *you*. The therapist supports you completely, no matter what you do—"

"Or *wear*...." Ted eyed Kate's hat with disdain.

"Or *eat*." Kate shoved Ted's sandwich, laden with corned beef and sauerkraut, a few inches farther down the table. "The point is, it gives you strength. You let Carly—and Judy for that matter—affect you too much. You need to find out what *you* want."

Ever since Kate had entered therapy a year ago, ostensibly to help her deal with her father's sudden death, she'd been a staunch advocate of the process. I knew that. I guess I wanted her to convince me one more time.

"Right now, I'm just so confused over Natalie. I keep trying to remember her, the things we did together, but I can't. I just want to be able to hold onto some part of her. But it's like she's slipped away...."

Kate nodded.

"I know how that is. A few weeks after my father died, I was staying with Mom and she woke up screaming one night. She said she couldn't remember Dad's face. She was completely hysterical, I couldn't calm her down. Finally, we went and got out some old photo albums and looked through them. It was the middle of the night, and we were sitting on the floor in the living room looking at pictures of their trips to Florida. She told me things about him she'd never told me before. I felt really close to him that night. So did she, I think."

Ted held his Perrier bottle to his mouth like a microphone. "Kate Heraden, your father just died. What are you going to do now?" He grabbed her hat and slapped it on his head. In a jittery falsetto, he screamed, "I'm going to DISNEYWORLD!"

They wrestled over the hat and I tossed a few more chunks of croissant at the crowd of sparrows now gathered at my feet.

Kate pushed her shoulder-length hair back into the hat. "Maybe you should try to find some pictures of Natalie? You must have some somewhere."

I thought of Mom's attic, the boxes we'd hauled up there and labelled in great detail the day she moved in. I seemed to remember several filled with things of mine from my childhood.

"I know Mom has some stuff I packed away when I went to college. Maybe I have some pictures of Natalie in there."

"Perfect. One problem solved. Now you just have to call this therapist and make an appointment."

* * * * *

"Hey, Mom, it's me."

"Emma? Where have you been, I tried calling you an hour ago."

"Sorry, we had a crisis at work. The printer lost some of the artwork for the July *Perspective*. We have to recreate sixteen pages by Friday."

"Is that very difficult?"

"Let's just say it's going to be a long week."

"The rewards of management. I'm proud of you, you know."

"Thanks. Listen, I was wondering if I could come over and go through the stuff in the attic. I wanted to see if I have any pictures of Natalie in my boxes up there."

"My God, I haven't been up there in years. It must be a disaster area. Sure, but let's make it tomorrow. I have a raging headache. I spent all day on the phone with Felicia. That woman's going to be the death of me."

"What's happening now?"

I pulled the phone to the couch and leaned back, familiar with the tone in Mom's voice that always preludes a long, and probably very funny, story.

"I don't want to talk about it. We've narrowed it down to two possible sites for the fund-raiser and she can't decide between them. The Landmark is okay, but parking stinks and the food is inedible. So I said the Sheraton. Good-size ballroom, the food's about what you'd expect, and they'll throw in fifty bottles of booze for free. But noooooo, Felicia says the drapes will clash with her color scheme."

"What's the color scheme?"

"Don't ask. 'Lemon meringue.'"

"What?"

"You heard me. She bought a pie and matched the colors of the filling and the meringue to little paint chips she's been carrying around in her purse. She wants to fill the place with daisies and give boutonnieres to all the guests."

"Won't that be expensive?"

"Oh, she isn't worried about that. She's completely forgotten this is a fund-raiser. She's trying to rival the Bush inauguration. Can you imagine men standing around with daisies stuck in their lapels? It'll look like a clown convention."

"So what's all this got to do with the drapes?"

"They're orange. Yellow, white and orange. She says it'll look like the place is on fire."

Mom's call waiting beeped and she put me on hold. I flicked on the TV and watched a few minutes of *The Wonder Years* in silence. Here was a man who remembered every detail of his childhood, down to what he had for dinner the night his mother lost the tax receipts. What was wrong with me?

"Emma? That was Felicia again. She bought another pie. Pumpkin. She's talking about giving the whole thing a Thanksgiving theme complete with turkeys and pilgrims and a real-life Indian."

"In August?"

"I'm telling you, I'm thinking about doing something desperate."

"Good luck."

"Thanks. Listen, I wanted to tell you I talked to Angela tonight. That's why I tried to call you earlier."

I turned off the TV and sat forward, picking up a pen and the envelope my phone bill came in.

I wrote: *Mom/Conversation with A 6/7/90* across the top. Don't ask me why.

"So what did she say?"

"She sounded better—the child abuse thing has been dropped, thank God. Now they're asking a lot of questions about Frank."

"What did they want to know?"

"She said they kept asking about his 'character,' whatever that means. They asked if Natalie was always as reluctant to go visit him as she was the day that false abuse report was filed. You know, when Angela had to practically force her into the car."

"What did Angela say?"

"She didn't tell me. She's pretty sure Frank's the one, though. He's been hanging around their house lately, trying to see her. Robert's working on getting a restraining order."

"What do you suppose Frank wants?"

"Whatever it is, he's adamant. He punched that Bennett shrimp in the face last night. Spent the night in jail for it."

"You're kidding!"

"Absolutely not. As far as Angela knows, he's still cooling his heels downtown. She doesn't think he has the money for bail. Bennett's pressing charges."

"Scary. But at least he can't harass her for awhile. I wouldn't want him hanging around my house."

"You said it. Listen, sweetheart, I've got to go. I told Felicia I'd call her back with my thoughts on the Thanksgiving idea."

"I'll see you tomorrow then about seven?"

"I'll fix something for dinner. You get some sleep, honey. I love you."

"I love you, too, Mom."

I hung up, looking at my notes about Mom's phone call with Angela. Everything seemed to point to Frank, but I still couldn't figure out why he hadn't left town. What did he want with Angela? Money? Or maybe Angela knew something. Maybe he wanted to make sure she couldn't tell anyone.

I rubbed my eyes, tired from sitting all afternoon in front of the computer. This whole situation was getting ridiculous. All I wanted was to remember Natalie and find out what happened to her. For my own peace of mind. Mercer's behavior, everyone's suspicions of him, forced me to think about how Natalie had died. The coroner's report said she probably suffocated...

My hand at my throat, I looked at my distorted reflection in the darkened television screen. I'd never thought about death much. I pictured Natalie fighting to breathe, unconsciously holding my own breath. In moments my lungs burned, painful pressure building behind my eyes. I exhaled loudly, gulping.

Chapter 16

"It's suffocating in here."

Mom wove among the piles of dusty boxes and moved a table lamp in front of the small attic window, setting it carefully on a stack of boxes marked LINENS. She fumbled with the latch and pushed with all her weight against the frame. The window didn't budge.

"Emma, give me a hand. I think it's painted shut."

I squeezed between the wall and a table covered with a dingy sheet. Together we pushed, and the window gave way with a sharp crack and a hideous screeching sound. Mom leaned into the screen, letting the breeze from outside fan her face. She had wrapped an old scarf over her hair and had on gardening gloves, but she still wore the tiny pearl earrings she'd put on for work.

Dusting the front of her work shirt, she scanned the dim space.

"We need some light. I don't suppose there's a plug up here."

As she hunted along the baseboards for an outlet, I picked among the boxes, looking for the ones I'd packed before going to college. The attic was really no more than a small storage space, accessed by a ladder that dropped through the ceiling into the second-floor hallway. The roof sloped to a point slightly off center, and I had to duck to avoid the heavy wooden support beams.

Behind me the lamp came to life, casting a yellow glow over the layer of dust that covered everything in sight. Mom gasped.

"This is disgusting—how could I have let this get so filthy?"

She drew a gloved finger across the nearest box, glaring at the trail it left behind.

"Mom, it's an attic. It isn't supposed to be clean."

"Clean is one thing. This is a nightmare. Where did I put that dustrag...."

While she fanned ten years of debris into the air, I pushed boxes aside, reading the lists of contents she'd written on each box in black capital letters. Most of the cartons contained things left over from my grandfather's house—kitchen utensils, books and other items she'd had no room for downstairs. I found an unmarked box and cleared a space for it on the floor.

"Did you find it?" Mom wiped her face with the rag, leaving a dark stripe of dirt across her forehead.

"I don't know. This one isn't labelled."

She bent over me as I slit the masking tape with a utility knife. Lifting the side, I pulled out a manila file folder that rested on top of what looked like business papers and account books. I opened the folder so Mom could see, as well.

"My God, this must be Daddy's."

She took the file and sat down beside me, flipping through the neatly typed pages with a wondering look on her face.

"*My* daddy's?" I couldn't believe she'd kept anything belonging to my father, and I wondered at my own sudden interest in him.

"No, no. *My* father's. After the house sold, there were some boxes of his I just couldn't bring myself to go through. I kept meaning to, but I guess I never got around to it. I'm sure there must be more around here. Look, these are copies of the letters he wrote to the Washington Post. My God, dozens of them. Vietnam, Nixon, Watergate.... I wonder if they were ever published?" She set the file folder on the floor and began sorting through the contents of the box.

I realized I was disappointed. For that split second, when I thought the papers belonged to my own father, my heart had lifted in anticipation. Mom didn't talk about him much, just that he'd been in the Navy and had wanted to be a journalist. Other than a few minor details, I didn't know him. I hadn't realized until now how much I wanted to.

"Oh, Emma, look. This must have been when my parents went to Scotland." She opened a small photograph album filled with faded square snapshots of my grandmother in front of a castle, a bridge, and various other landmarks. I peered at the woman in the pictures.

"You look so much like her." I handed the album back to Mom.

"Yes, I guess I do. I remember going to Seattle once with my father to visit his sister. He was unloading the bags and I walked up to the house. Aunt Edith came out and threw her arms around me, saying 'Why Ruth, you haven't changed a bit.'" She laughed at the memory, but there was a sadness in her eyes. Opening the album to the only close-up picture of her mother, Mom traced the outline of her face lightly.

"You know I don't even remember her. I was twelve when she died, and yet I can't remember her at all. It's almost as if I've erased her from my childhood. I can see my father there, and my sister, but I can't see her. Isn't that strange...."

I didn't know what to say. She seemed more puzzled than anything else. I reached into the box and pulled out a framed photograph, taken in a lush country garden. The sun was shining brightly on the group, and my grandmother held a hand up to Mom's forehead to shade her eyes. In the background, someone sat in a lawn chair beneath a shady tree. Mom took the frame and dusted the glass with her hand.

"That's Aunt Edith in the background, with Emma in her lap. She had such a lovely garden. Just look at the wisteria! I must have been nine when this was taken, and Emma was seven. You look so much like her."

I smiled, wishing again I'd known my namesake. Mom's sister died at eighteen, of a hemorrhage. An illegal abortion. Mom told me once that the greatest tragedy about Aunt Emma's death was that my grandfather would have been willing to help her find a competent doctor. Up until he died, he'd been a staunch supporter of a woman's right to choose. But Emma had been young and afraid. Convinced she was all alone, she'd gone to Philadelphia and died in a motel room, alone.

When I was fourteen, my grandfather sat me down and told me the story. He ended it by saying, 'Emma, I know you're still young, but you're growing up fast. I can't tell you what choices to make in your life, but if you ever need help with anything, you come to me. You must always remember that you're not alone. You have your mother and me, and we'll always be there for you. Promise me.' At the time, I'd been frightened by the gravity in his voice. I swore I'd always tell him if I needed anything. Then he crushed me in his huge arms, and cried.

"Well, I should go through this later." Mom packed everything back into the box and set it near the ladder. I stood and faced her, still feeling my grandfather's strong back heaving in grief.

"Mom...."

She turned to me, pushing a loose strand of hair into her scarf.

"Yes? Honey, what is it?" She came to me and put a hand on my arm.

"I was just remembering Grandpa. He died when I was twelve. Do you think I'll forget him, too?"

She pulled me to her, patting the back of my head. "Oh, honey, no. You just have to keep remembering him. He's always there." She pulled away and looked into my eyes. "Don't worry, sweetheart. Listen, why don't we go through his boxes together. You can take whatever you want. Okay?"

I nodded. I thought of the poem he kept on his wall, Robert Frost's "The Road Not Taken." Maybe that was here somewhere. I wanted that.

"Now, let's find those photographs for you."

She handed me several small boxes marked FRAGILE, containing her vast collection of Christmas ornaments and decorations. I piled them off to one side, placing them gently on the floor. I'd once estimated that her collection was worth upwards of $25,000. Decorating her Christmas tree was something I looked forward to all year.

Outside the tiny window, sunlight pelted the awning in the backyard of the house next door. The red stripes melted away, while the white stripes seemed to sway and pulse in the heat. Six months till Christmas. Oh well.

"Here we go! Just as I thought." Mom indicated two book-size boxes with pride. We each took one and set them in the center of the attic.

Mom sliced through the tape on one of the boxes and spread the lid open. Wadded newspaper formed a protective cushion across the top, revealing nothing inside. She pulled out an oblong object and began peeling the paper off.

"Good Lord, Emma, why on earth did you save this?"

She glared at the trophy I'd won in high school for giving a speech before the Association of Teachers of English.

"What do you mean?" I grabbed it from her, admiring the gold plastic statuette of a man in full academic regalia. A brass plate at the base of the trophy read 'Emma Kendrick, FOURTH PLACE, ATE Speech Competition 1982.' "I *earned* this trophy."

"Oh, well, pardon me. Perhaps there's a place for it on your mantle." She laughed. I set in on the floor, fully planning to throw it away at the first opportunity.

Sitting side by side, we unwrapped the odds and ends of my high school career, Mom trying in vain to control the growing mass of crinkled newspaper piling up between us. The box contained wine glasses from my Senior Prom, a lot of the ceramic figurines and knick knacks that used to litter the shelves in my room and not much else. We had nearly reached the bottom of the box when Mom came across a silver heart-shaped jewelry box lined in grey felt.

"Where did you get this?" She turned it over in her hands.

"I think Grandpa gave it to me."

"He must have. This was Emma's. I remember she kept it on her dresser. I think Aunt Edith gave it to her."

She handed it to me, and I held the jewelry box in both hands, watching the light play off the tarnished silver lid. It was heavy, with three little carved feet that poked into my palms. I pressed my hands to it and felt the cold metal warm to my touch. Aunt Emma's jewelry box. Instantly, it became my most-prized possession.

"Well, at least there's something here worth keeping." Mom pulled the other box toward her. "This one weighs a ton. Hand me the knife."

As Mom cut through the bindings, I read the side of the box, where I'd listed, in my best scrawling penmanship, what was inside. Yearbooks, letters, scrapbooks, pictures, 'memerabilia' (the editor in me shuddered) and diaries. I slammed a hand over the lid before Mom could open the box.

"What's wrong?"

"Um, I think I want to open this one alone."

"Why? Uh-oh, something here your old Mom can't see?" She turned the box so she could read the list of contents. "Yearbooks, letters, pictures, what's so bad about—oh, *diaries.* I see. What's in them? Some vitriolic tirades about your poor mother?" Her eyes gleamed with amusement.

"No, I just want to look at them first, okay?"

She smiled and pushed herself into a standing position, dusting off the knees of her jeans.

"I understand. I'd better get downstairs anyway. Felicia's supposed to call, and I have to work up the courage to tell her I signed the Sheraton contract today. She wanted them to include a paragraph stating they'd allow a live elephant in the ballroom *and* clean up after it. Needless to say, they wouldn't."

"A live elephant, what's that got to do with Thanksgiving?"

"Oh, we're not doing Thanksgiving anymore. Thank God I talked her out of that. Now it's a circus theme. Felicia's hunting for a trapeze act as we speak. Can you imagine? The ceiling's only eighteen feet tall. She wants the waiters to dress in costume, too. If she doesn't bankrupt the Commission before this is over, I'll do a triple somersault without a net myself."

* * * * *

When I finally kicked the boxes through the door to my apartment, I collapsed against the wall in exhaustion. Heading for the kitchen and a much-needed Diet Pepsi, I hit the playback on my answering machine.

"Yo, Adriane!" Carly's voice reverberated off the walls. "Darling, angel, best-friend-a-girl-could-ever-have, I need your help. I found a couple of jobs that look like possible improvements over the Hell I'm Living Now, but my resumé sucks. Can you come over, my wonderful, favorite, brilliant, gorgeous Editor-Extraordinaire, and fix it tomorrow? Leftover chili—yum-yum-yum! I didn't even put garlic in it, I swear. PLEASE PLEASE PLEASE??? I'm headed for yet another GLuRCk fund-raiser meeting—this is number 7,459—so leave a message on my machine. By the way, Pat's hot for your body. Yeow-sa!"

I dialed Carly's number, listened to her latest message, something about winning the lottery and running off to Paris with Michelle Pfeiffer, and said I'd be there at seven. I knew I had no other choice—if I didn't show up, she'd come to me. I was far from keen on facilitating Carly's job hunt, but I also felt mildly guilty for being so selfish. She hated her job, and maybe one of these new opportunities was in Washington. I held on to that sliver of hope and plunked myself down on the floor.

Sitting spread eagle in front of the coffee table, I pulled the box with the diaries in it between my legs. On top lay a stack of letters bound in pink ribbon, all the return addresses reading Milwaukee, Wisconsin. I laughed out loud, remembering my great love, Mickey, from summer camp the year before I started high school. He was six inches shorter than me, and we'd only 'fallen in love' because all the other campers in our group had already paired off. In retrospect, I'm sure he was gay. I put the letters aside, thinking I'd read them for hidden signals later.

I piled the old books I'd saved onto the coffee table, alongside several loose photographs of high school friends. The bulk of the box was taken up by four yearbooks, bound in green and gold, and signed in juvenile handwriting by people I couldn't remember at all.

I found the diaries stacked in a corner of the box. There were seven of them, varying in size from the typical small volume with a lock glued onto the cover to three larger, fabric-covered blank books I'd used in high school. The one I wanted was small, bound in red vinyl and locked, although I had no trouble opening it.

The inside cover read *Emma Kendrick 1973*, in fat, carefully drawn letters. Each page began with the day and date, but I hadn't started writing in it until April 27, my eighth birthday.

April 27
Dear Diary,
 Today I got up and ate cereal for breakfast. Natalie and me went roller skating in the apartments. We had lunch at Natalie's house. Meatloaf sandwiches. Then Mom watched us at the pool. Then I went home. Natalie and her Mom came over for dinner for my birthday. We had chocolate cake and spaghetti. I got a dress that is yellow and this diary from my Mom. It was a nice day.

May 14
Dear Diary,
 Natalie got a new bike from Mr. Campbell today, so we went bike riding to the park and played on the swings. Natalie asked me to spend the night, but her Mom said I couldn't. We are going to the pool tomorrow with Stacy and Heidi and their Mom.

Some entries mentioned Natalie kissing me. I read them carefully, wondering at how easily I'd accepted—and enjoyed—kissing her. I'd never questioned it. Somehow this made me proud. Guess I'd been a lesbian at heart all along.

June 4
Dear Diary,

Natalie and me played house at the terrace today after school. She played the Dad and I played the Mom. She came home from work and kissed me and then we ate dinner. Then she put the babies to sleep and I washed dishes. Then we went to bed and kissed some more. It was fun.

The pages continued in a similar vein. I couldn't remember doing any of the things the diary described. Nearly every page was filled with stories about trips to the zoo, day camp crafts at the local church, swimming at the pool—two blocks from the complex. I'd taken life-saving lessons there several years later. My certificate rested on the coffee table beside the books and photographs, another of the things I'd found in the box.

Few of my diary entries shed any insight into Natalie's life, until I reached October, the month before Natalie disappeared.

October 30
Dear Diary,

Today at school we had a Halloween party. Miss Shaw gave us crayons and paper and we made Halloween masks and then we had candy. Natalie traded me for the ones with coconut in them that make me itch. Tomorrow, Mommy is taking me trick-or-treating but Natalie can't go because she has to go see her Dad. Natalie said she probably won't get to go trick-or-treating so I have to save some candy for her. I think she is sad.

November 2
Dear Diary,

Today Natalie was in trouble, so we didn't play at the terrace after school. I watched cartoons. I asked Mommy why Natalie was in trouble and she said she didn't know. It seems like Nata-

*lie always gets in trouble when she goes to see her Dad. I don't
think she should go there anymore.*

When I turned the page, I saw that I'd written an entry on
the last night Natalie was ever seen.

November 14
Dear Diary,
*Natalie was very sad today. I think we're going to run away
tomorrow. She said she has to go see her Dad again this weekend
and she doesn't want to. I wanted to tell my Mommy that we are
running away, but Natalie told me not to. I am supposed to bring
cookies for us to eat. I will also bring my diary so I can write in it
if we don't get back in time.*

That was the last entry in the diary. I closed it, holding it
against my chest and fighting tears. For the first time, I remembered that night. Natalie had been upset all day, planning to
run away and begging me to come with her. I didn't know where
we were going, but Natalie seemed to have some place in mind.
She wouldn't tell me what was wrong, but I trusted her, completely. I remembered sneaking into the kitchen and stealing a
bag of Oreos in preparation for our trip. I hid them under my
bed, and kept checking to make sure they were still there all
night long.

The next day, as police cars gathered around Natalie's house,
my mother kept me inside, occasionally peeking out the window
to see what was going on. When the detective came to ask her
questions, I slipped out the back and ran to the terrace. In our
fort, I cried angry tears, sure that Natalie had run away without
me. Why had she left without me? What had I done?

I remembered huddling in the fort until night fell; then I
emerged to hear my mother screaming my name from the parking lot above the terrace. I climbed up the pitted hillside and
squeezed through the fence, appearing behind her and tugging

at her skirt. She whipped around and embraced me, crying and yelling at the same time. She'd been terrified that I'd been abducted too.

Now I understood the fear she must have suffered that day, unable to find me, watching the terrible drama unfold at the Campbell's. It took a long time for me to understand what had happened to Natalie. I remained convinced she had run away, and frantically tried to imagine where she would have gone. I waited long hours in our fort, listening for the sound of her shoes scraping against the giant steps. She never came.

I replaced the things that I wanted to keep in the box, shoving it into a closet with my trophy. It was nearly eleven-thirty and my eyes ached from reading. I hadn't found any pictures of Natalie, but her face was everywhere around me. I shut out the lights and lay back on the couch, reliving those last few hours before Natalie had disappeared.

What had happened that night? Frank must have been right beneath my window before Mrs. Huntemann scared him off. In a dream, I saw Natalie come downstairs and open the front door, to stand in the doorway in her nightgown. Frank approached and tried to convince her to come with him. She told him no and he grabbed her, clapping a hand over her mouth to stifle her screams. He shook her, her eyes wide with terror, his hand closing off her breathing passages. She clawed at his wrists, kicking him through the thin fabric of her nightgown. Then she went limp.

137

Chapter 17

Rain pounded the Celica as I pulled into the apartment building's flooded parking lot Thursday night. Lightning periodically lit the sky like so many flashbulbs at a press conference. I opened the car door and stepped out, my left foot sinking below the greasy surface of a large puddle. I huddled against the driving wind and ducked through the glass doors into the lobby. The rain abated just as I pressed the elevator button. The perfect end to a perfect day.

That morning, I'd woken to the sound of a garbage truck emptying the giant brown dumpsters in back of my building. It was a sound I'd never heard before—a very *loud* sound accompanied by workers yelling at each other and the persistent beeping of the truck's alarm as it backed into place. I'd never heard it before because the garbage people don't arrive until after 9:00 a.m., long past when I'm supposed to be at work.

I jumped off the couch, still wearing what I'd worn the day before and clutching my diary from 1973. Rushing around, I'd managed to shower, dress and slam the door behind me in less than twenty minutes.

At work, I'd moved even faster, trying to recreate the missing pages from *Perspective*. It was an all-out effort, everyone in the Women's Department rushing about in a frenzy, and others volunteering to help with the paste-up. The magazine was nearly complete now, except for a few photos, three ads and the first page of the monthly calendar of events, which no one seemed willing to admit they'd put together in the first place. Now, almost twelve hours later, I had a headache that started behind my eyes and spread to my lower back, and I still had to help Carly with her resumé.

In the elevator riding up to my apartment, I listened to the monotonous drip-drip-drip coming off my clothes and umbrella. All I wanted was a hot cup of tea and to curl under a blanket and go to sleep. I wasn't hungry: I'd called Carly and canceled dinner two hours ago. I wanted to avoid going there entirely, but I didn't know how. I already felt guilty enough for not supporting her job search, one night wouldn't hurt. Tomorrow was Friday, I could rest then.

Two of the light fixtures mounted on the walls of the 10th-floor hallway were out, leaving eerie pools of shadow outside the elevator and directly in front of my door. I noticed my neighbor hadn't yet picked up his morning newspaper and wondered vaguely where he was this time. Wherever he was, I hoped he'd remembered to turn down the volume on his answering machine. The last thing I needed was to spend another night listening to people leave him bizarre messages at the top of their lungs.

All right, I was in a bad mood. You know how it is. You wake up late and nothing goes right all day. I'd no sooner gotten Belinda Blake's fluff piece on the First Lady pasted up when someone spilled half a cup of coffee all over the artwork. Four hours' work dripping with decaf. And that was just the beginning. At four-thirty, the thunderstorms no one had predicted wiped out our computer system, obliterating two other pieces and some of the work already done on the August issue. Now I couldn't find my keys in the bottom of my bag. I wanted to scream.

I wanted to cry.

Finally, I found my key chain, but couldn't manage to isolate the two particular keys needed to open my door. I set my bag against the door momentarily and stopped short when the door separated from the frame at the slight pressure.

My heart pounding, my aggravation replaced with animal fear, I nudged the door fully open and peered inside. The apartment was completely dark, except for the red light on my answering machine, which blinked silently across the room. I listened for breathing or footsteps, but didn't hear anything other than my own elevated pulse. Entering cautiously, I threw on the lights in the living room and gripped the handle of my umbrella like a baseball bat.

I know I should have turned and run. Everything in me told me to do just that, but I pressed on. I pictured my obituary in the paper the next day alongside a lengthy article about how women can avoid victimization if they just keep their wits about them, scream for help, and then run *away* from danger.

I left the front door open, hoping whoever was inside would take it into his heart to leave the way he had come. Breathlessly I yanked open closet doors and whipped the shower curtain aside. By the time I reached the kitchen, every light in the place was burning. Nothing was missing. What was going on?

Flipping on the harsh fluorescent light in the kitchen, I thrust the umbrella forward, scaring myself and two cockroaches who'd been munching on a potato chip near the refrigerator. On the counter, a pink piece of paper lay by the sink. I could see the writing from the doorway.

"SOMEONE WAS IN YOUR APARTMENT." I recognized my landlord's nearly illegible scrawl. He'd added "Checked screens for window washing."

When I could breathe calmly again, I played back my phone messages, and changed into jeans and a sweatshirt. Casting a longing look at my bed, I hoped Carly's resumé rewrite wouldn't take long.

"Emma? Hello, Emma honey, this is Dorothy Huntemann. I'm callin' from my friend Florence's place—what? No Florence, I'm talkin' to Emma's machine, she's not there. You sit down, dinner's almost ready. I just have to fix up the potatoes and we'll eat, all right? Emma? It's me again—that was Florence just now.

Thought I was talkin' to you, she did. She gets a little impatient when she's hungry. I'm fixin' us some pork chops and mashed potatoes, you know, and they smell pretty good, if I do say so myself. No, Florence, sit at the table, honey, we'll eat soon's I'm done talkin' to Emma's machine. Now where was I? Oh, yes. I wanted to call you and see how you're doin' and if you talked to that Joyce yet. Like I said, I'm here with Florence today and we were talkin' about the tragedy with that poor little girl and all, and would you believe, Florence told me the strangest thing. I won't tell you now, I know these machine's don't let you talk for very long, but it's somethin' I think you should hear. So I thought, why not have you down to dinner and I'll have Florence tell you herself? No, honey, I'm still talkin' to Emma. So you come by around seven, Emma, and I'll fix us some chicken. You're not a vegetarian, are you? That's fine if you are, I can always whip up a salad. You just come by around seven. We'll see you then. Goodbye!"

Mrs. Huntemann said something to Florence as she hung up, and the machine beeped. So much for my Friday night off. I paused beside the desk waiting for the second message to begin. I crossed my fingers it was Carly saying I didn't have to come over.

I waited, but no one spoke. Turning up the volume, I could hear music in the background and the slight hiss of someone breathing, but he didn't say anything. Just when I thought I'd identified the music, he hung up and my machine beeped again, three short bursts, indicating I had no more messages. I considered replaying the message, but it was getting late and I wanted to get over to Carly's before it started raining again.

Resetting the machine, I shivered, suddenly glad for a reason to leave.

* * * * *

"So they didn't say anything?" Carly poured me a glass of mineral water and handed it to me on our way into the den.

"No. Just breathing. I thought I recognized the music in the

141

background, but now I can't remember what it was."

"God, I hate that. What does it take to leave a message? I remember when I came back from that camping trip there were sixteen messages on my machine and eight of them were hang-ups. God, I wanted to kill them."

Carly pulled her wild hair into a ponytail and punched a few buttons on the computer. It whirred to life, displaying a series of numbers and letters across the screen.

"It's just so weird, you know? First the door's open, then there's a breather on my answering machine.... It's like someone's watching me."

I sat on a chair near the computer and sipped my water, watching Carly's stubby fingers race across the keyboard, calling up her resumé.

"I can't believe they can just walk into your apartment without asking."

"It's in my lease. 'Unrestricted access as needed for purposes of building maintenance.'"

"Bullshit. I'd tell them to go to hell. Here it is."

She got up and I took her seat in front of the computer. She stood behind me, her face reflected in the screen.

"Now I know it isn't perfect, but just tell me what you think. I want to sound like I know what I'm talking about but I don't want to make it seem like I'm just a computer jock."

I read the resumé, starting with her name in bold capitals centered at the top: CARLOTTA M. VELASQUEZ. I snickered in spite of myself. She just doesn't look like a "Carlotta."

"Shut up and read." She hit the back of my head and stalked out, her hair bouncing behind her.

I made a few cursory edits to the two-page document, feeling my stomach tighten as I read. It was an impressive resumé and clearly showed Carly knows her stuff when it comes to programming and setting up sophisticated computer models. I didn't understand most of it, but I was sure that anyone who did know computers would want to interview her. I saved the file and sent through a print command, getting up to join her in the living room.

"Looks fine. I just changed a few things to make it parallel."

"Whatever that means. God, I hope I find something soon. I can't take it much longer." She pulled her hair out of the rubber band and ran her fingers through it, leaning back on the couch against Ruby's fluffy form. Ruby, stretched across the back of the couch, snorted as Carly's hair splayed over her face.

"Get this. Today, I was in the computer room working on some code. Asswipe Bernie comes in and starts rubbing my shoulders with his clammy hands. I told him to keep them to himself and he says, 'You know, the right man could change your mind.'"

"You've got to be kidding."

"I'm absolutely serious. I went to Adelson and he told me there was nothing he could do, that this was a 'personality conflict' and I should take care of it myself."

"It's sexual harassment!"

"No shit. But it's such a boys' club down there. God, sometimes I just want to ram a fist down someone's throat. I'm doing the work of three people and getting paid shit for it.... It's just so fucking frustrating."

I watched her yanking her hair out by the roots and didn't know what to do. She reminded me so much of Judy—intelligent, dedicated and shot down time and time again by short-sighted employers who still see women as secretaries and baby factories. One had even told Judy he didn't want to promote her because the minute he did, she'd get married and leave. It didn't matter that she'd told him she was a lesbian, he considered that a temporary state.

"I don't want to talk about this anymore. I've just got to send out some resumés and find another job. I know it's out there, I just have to find it."

She sat forward, determination hardening the lines of her face. Turning to me, her eyes widened a little, as if she was surprised to see me sitting there.

"So what's up with you? How's work?" She slapped my thigh and headed into the den to retrieve her printed resumé.

"Busy. We're still trying to piece together the July issue. I was there till 9:00 tonight."

"How's Kate? I keep meaning to call and invite her to go with us to see Ms. Clinton. Linda canceled, she's going to New York that weekend with some woman she met at work."

Carly emerged from the den, scrutinizing her resumé and nodding in agreement with my changes.

"She's fine. We had lunch yesterday. She said I should think about going into therapy."

She looked up and frowned, setting the papers on the back of the couch. Ruby eyed them suspiciously.

"God, not that again. Emma, I'm telling you, it's a waste of time."

I watched her walk to the dining room table and pick up some papers, her back to me. Tired, I didn't think before I spoke.

"Why do you keep saying that? Kate said it really helped her deal with her father's death."

Carly turned around and leaned against the table, the papers still in her hand. She took a deep breath.

"I was in therapy once myself, all right? It sucked."

"Why? You never told me."

"It doesn't matter why. I went to this woman in college a few times, I started to fall in love with her, she told me I was 'transferring repressed feelings of hostility toward my mother' and I never went back. I don't want to talk about it."

Carly kept her eyes on her papers, shuffling them around the table and distractedly placing them in piles. Then she changed the subject.

"How's the investigation going? You still playing Nancy Drew?" Her tone was light, facetious, indicating the tension was over and she wasn't angry with me.

"Mrs. Huntemann called me tonight. She said her friend

Florence found out something. Florence lives in the same building as Joyce Slocombe."

"Jesus, Emma, I was kidding. You're really still trying to figure out who did it?"

"She just said she had something to tell me, that's all. It may not even be about Natalie."

"Just be careful, all right?"

Carly really seemed worried that I'd get hurt. I thought about how I'd reacted to the open door and the message on my machine. Maybe I was getting in over my head.

"I will. It's just dinner."

"So have the police arrested what's-her-name, the mom, yet?"

I joined her at the table, Carly still sorting her papers into neat piles. I saw they were notes about job listings and a flyer from some west coast association about job opportunities for women in the computer field.

"No, they dropped that. My mother talked to her Tuesday night. I guess they're moving in on Frank Mercer now."

"You think he did it?"

"I don't know. I have this weird feeling that Bobbie's involved somehow."

"Bobbie?"

"Natalie's younger sister. She just graduated from college. I'm not sure why, but I feel like she knows something."

"How? She couldn't have been more than three years old when Natalie disappeared."

"I know. I just get this weird feeling when I see her."

Carly looked up from her papers and a slow smile spread across her face.

"You're hot for her, aren't you."

It was a statement, not a question. An uneasy warmth spread up my arms and across my face.

"No, I'm not. I just think she knows something about Natalie's death."

"Emma! You're turning beet red! I can't believe it. You think she's a dyke?"

"I don't know. It's possible. You know how they say you can tell a lesbian by whether she looks you straight in the eye? Bobbie does that."

Carly whistled through her teeth.

"So what's she like? Are you going to go for it?"

"No!"

"Wait a minute. You're not still holding out on account of Judy are you?"

"What? No...."

"Emma, you have to go on with your life. Judy's history. If you're attracted to Bobbie, go for it. You won't be cheating on Judy, I'm sure she's already found several warm bodies to share her sleeping bag with."

Carly's indictment of Judy aside, I realized she was partly right. The feelings Bobbie engendered in me were close to guilt. But was it about Judy? Or Natalie...? I didn't want to talk about it anymore. I wanted to go home.

"Well it doesn't matter anyway, because it isn't going to happen. I just thought she knew something about Natalie's death."

Carly stacked her papers and shoved them into a file folder, in turn putting the folder in her leather carry-all. "Listen, Emma, you're getting obsessed with this Natalie thing. I really think you should let it go."

At that, something in me snapped.

"Carly, you don't understand. I have to know what happened. She was my best friend. I have to know why she died."

"For God's sake, Emma, it was seventeen years ago!"

"That doesn't mean I don't still miss her."

"How can you miss someone you haven't seen in seventeen years?"

Anger flashed through me. "Maybe I care about my friends a little more than you do."

She stared at me, her hand still inside the brief case. "What's that supposed to mean?"

Tears welled in my eyes. "I just don't think it would be as easy for me to pick up and move away."

Carly's eyes seemed opaque, devoid of feeling. "Emma, I can't stay here just because you want me to. I need to make a career move. You're being selfish."

"I'm sorry! I'm just sick of watching people leave. I don't understand why it's selfish of me to want the people I love to stay near me. Why isn't it selfish of you to move away just to get a better job?"

"You can't cling to people like that, Emma. You have to let them go."

"I can't! God, why don't you understand? Please, Natalie, don't go!"

Something transformed her features. Her mouth fell slightly open and she stiffened. "Emma, you called me Natalie."

I panicked, feeling a cold chill up my spine. I had to escape.

Somehow, I found myself outside, on Carly's porch. The rain pelted my face and hands. A flash of lightning lit the sky and framed the Celica. I headed toward it, somewhere in the back of my mind hoping Carly would stop me. But she didn't. I gunned the engine, taking one last look at the house. Carly wasn't at any of the windows.

She was already gone.

Chapter 18

Natalie squatted on the ground, poking a stick at something crawling among the rocks of the creek bed. I sat a few feet away, my back against the lowest terrace step, watching her. Closing one eye, I traced her silhouette with the stick in my hand.

"When do you leave?"

She pried a stone loose and jabbed the damp earth beneath. "Friday. Daddy's picking me up after school."

She stood, tossing her stick on the ground and wiping her hands on her shorts.

"I wish you didn't have to go."

She stood in front of me and grabbed the end of my stick, swinging it back and forth to her own tempo. "Me too. I'm sorry."

I looked up at her. She chewed her lower lip thoughtfully, staring up the terrace steps behind me. Her nose and cheeks were sunburned, pink beneath the blue of her eyes.

The stultifying summer heat and humidity blanketed the suburbs, keeping everyone indoors, except restless little girls. We moved slowly, lazy in the summer sun. Even the creek bed, perennially in shadow, felt like an oven holding the heat in around us.

"How long this time?"

"A week. I come back on Sunday."

Natalie sat down beside me and fanned her face with the hem of her t-shirt. "I wouldn't go if I didn't have to."

"I know."

She leaned against the cool concrete. In my mind, I was already counting down the days till she'd return.

She held out her pinky, crooked to accept mine in solemn oath.

"Let's promise that when we grow up, we'll never go away."

I linked my finger with hers.

"Promise."

We sat at the base of the terrace, pinkies interlocked, watching a sultry breeze play with the leaves of the eucalyptus.

Natalie rested her head against my shoulder. I sat very still, not wanting to disturb her. Even when my neck began to hurt and my arm got stiff and numb, I didn't complain. She was like a butterfly. I thought if I didn't move, she'd stay there forever.

Chapter 19

I pulled into the visitors' parking lot at Oakbrook, tired and not really looking forward to dinner at Mrs. Huntemann's.

Work had been hell. Just as we got the last ad in place, Hank the printer had called to say he'd found the missing *Perspective* flats. They were on his desk the whole time—buried under a pile of take-out menus, if you can believe that. After Merry got done disemboweling him over the phone, Ted and one of the graphic artists put together a life-size caricature of Hank and we burned it in effigy behind the building. Of course, this wasn't until close to six o'clock. By that point, not even Hank in flames could improve my mood.

The missing pages didn't bother me nearly as much as my argument with Carly. I'd been trying to get in touch with her all day. I called her at home before I left for work and then every hour on the hour after that. I only succeeded in alienating the receptionist at her office who, the last time I called, asked if Carly owed me money.

I trudged the length of the driveway toward Mrs. Huntemann's house and stepped onto the pebbled walkway between my old house and Natalie's. The family now living in Natalie's house was at home, their drapes and windows open to the evening breeze.

The three of them sat on the floor playing a board game—a scene taken straight from the cover of the *Saturday Evening Post*. Dad, in a plaid shirt and jeans, stretched his arm across the sofa cushions, cradling Mom in her full-length peach-colored house dress. Baby Girl Perfect sat across from them, her face away from me. Achingly familiar white-blonde hair cascaded down her back, pulled away from her face by twin pink plastic barrettes. She moved the pieces on the game board like race cars, while Mom and Dad chuckled with amused pride and gave each other loving looks.

I realized I'd been staring at them for some time when the man's eyes met mine. He tilted his head in a gentle, questioning way, and Baby Girl turned to the window. Her blue-eyed stare shot through me like hot lead. I forced my feet forward, feeling the breeze cold against my face. I was shaking all over.

A split second after I knocked, Mrs. Huntemann opened the door with a wooden spoon held high in her left hand. I ducked instinctively, raising my arms in front of my face.

She apologized profusely, waving the spoon around and splattering the front of my shirt with something brown and syrupy that smelled wonderful. "Oh dear, I don't know why I did that. Florence? Florence, I just scared poor Emma here half to death. You see, I was walkin' into the kitchen—had this spoon in my hand, I did—and when she knocked, well I just opened the door without thinkin'! What with the spoon in my hand, why I must have looked like I was about to beat her senseless. I'm so sorry, honey. Really, I am."

She pressed me into a wing chair, shoving Tinkerbell onto the floor. "Now you just sit down and catch your breath, Emma honey, and I'll finish what I was doin' in the kitchen. Dinner's almost ready, I just have to steam the asparagus and take the bread out of the oven. Table's all set...now let's see—Florence, you're drinking sherry, I think you'll be fine for awhile. Emma? Can I get you somethin' to drink?"

I asked for a Diet Pepsi, offering to get it myself, but she patted my shoulder and assured me she didn't need any help. As she padded off to the kitchen, I turned to Florence and introduced myself.

151

She didn't hear me, though. From what Mrs. Huntemann had said about the sherry, the empty glass on the table in front of her and her deep, nasal breathing, I deduced Florence had overindulged and was now asleep. I settled back into the chair—ever-so-slowly so as not to further provoke Tinkerbell. Somehow I managed to cross my legs without upending any of the tables that surrounded my chair. In the warm embrace of Mrs. Huntemann's house, I began to relax immediately.

Florence snored lightly, her hands folded across her ample bosom. Her tightly-curled, strawberry-blonde wig listed slightly to the left. She smiled in her sleep, tiny dimples creasing her wrinkled cheeks. The sherry had tinted her nose a rosy pink, a color repeated in the stripes on her dress. If Mrs. Huntemann was primarily blue, Florence ran definitely toward the reds.

"Here we go, honey. I'm afraid I didn't have any Diet Pepsi—the store brand was on sale this week and I had a coupon. Twisted a lemon in it, shouldn't be too bad."

Florence stirred on the couch, her hair sliding even further down the side of her head. Mrs. Huntemann negotiated her way behind the couch and rearranged the wig, nudging Florence awake.

"Wha—? Dottie? Was I sleeping? Is it dinnertime?" Florence threw her head all the way back, speaking up at Mrs. Huntemann's down-turned face and causing the wig to fall behind the couch. Mrs. Huntemann bent to retrieve it, and Florence righted herself, blinking at me. Her real hair, a snowy white, looked much better than the wig.

"Who's that? Who are you? Dottie? Who's that sitting in your chair? Do I know you? Dottie? Do I know him?"

Mrs. Huntemann placed the wig back on Florence's head, leaning to speak in Florence's ear.

"This is Emma Kendrick, Florence. You remember, the one I told you about. Come for dinner, she has."

Florence squinted and pushed herself forward. Smiling, she extended a hand, palm down, and, with the other hand, pulled her hemline a few inches farther down her knees.

"So pleased to meet you, Elmer." She suddenly acquired a Mississippi accent. "Dottie's told me so much about you."

I shook her hand, although my instincts told me she expected it to be kissed.

"It's, uh, Emma. I'm happy to meet you, too, Ms.—" I glanced helplessly at Mrs. Huntemann.

"Florence, please. Known her seventy years, I have, and I still can't pronounce her last name. Florence?" She raised her voice, "Florence, dinner's on the table. You want to wash your hands or anythin' before we eat?"

Florence grunted, shaking her head, and reached out to me to help her rise. She was heavier than she looked, and I nearly fell into a sea of ceramic curios trying to pull her up. We trooped single-file into the dining room, pawing through a swag of colored beads, and were assailed by the heady aromas of fresh-baked bread and tarragon.

Mrs. Huntemann had outdone herself. The table sparkled under the weight of fine china, wine glasses, serving dishes and platters, all heaped with steaming delicacies. It was enough to feed us well into the next century. I sat down between the two women, wishing I still had an appetite and feeling guilty for not wanting to come. This dinner must have taken all day to prepare.

"Well, we're all here, thank heaven for that. Nothin's burnt, nobody's sick, and we made it through another day without blowin' each other up. Here's to one more."

I realized—too late—that Mrs. Huntemann was praying. We tipped glasses filled with cold white wine and Florence scanned the serving dishes, reaching halfway across the table to get first shot at the scalloped potatoes.

Throughout dinner, which I only nibbled but enjoyed because of the smell, Mrs. Huntemann dominated the conversation. I'm ashamed to say her knowledge of current events, far surpassing mine, took me by surprise. She and Florence argued the merits

153

of the pending civil rights bill and postulated at length on the effects of Medicare's new physician payment system. I contributed as much as I could, but in truth, I was way out of my league. I did sell two subscriptions to *Perspective,* though.

After barely making a dent in the food, we adjourned to the living room, where Mrs. Huntemann laid out rich-smelling coffee and buttery sugar cookies. Florence found room for both. I accepted coffee, heavily laced with whipping cream, and watched through the beaded curtain as Tinkerbell took her turn at the dinner table.

"Think I'll leave the dishes for tomorrow. Like my daddy used to say, 'The Lord won't come for you tonight if you got a sink full of dirty pots in the kitchen.'"

"But the bugs will." Florence popped another cookie in her mouth and gave me a crumbly grin.

Mrs. Huntemann pursed her lips. "Don't see you volunteerin' for KP."

"You want a dishwasher, buy one."

I interrupted what appeared to be a standard after dinner argument before it could come to blows. "Um, Mrs. Huntemann, when you called you said you had something to tell me?"

"Why, we were havin' such a nice time, I nearly forgot. Florence, tell Emma what you heard on Tuesday."

"You mean about my bunions? Doctor says I gotta quit wearing these shoes...." She lifted a foot and began to unbuckle a red sling-back sandal that was at least four sizes too small.

Mrs. Huntemann smacked Florence's foot to the floor. "No, no, *no!* Tell her what you told me yesterday—you know, how you heard that Joyce arguin' with somebody."

"Oh! Well, why didn't you say so in the first place." Florence settled back, nabbing several cookies for the trip.

"Well, I tell you she was *steaming.* Just shouting as loud as she could. I didn't even have to walk down the hall—I could hear her from my doorway."

I thought it wise not to ask what had prompted Florence to

open the door in the first place.

"Yes, yes, yes, but what did she *say*? Tell her what that Joyce said." Mrs. Huntemann prodded Florence by hitting her thigh with the back of her hand.

"Don't rush me, Dottie, I'm getting to that. Now let's see, the first thing I heard was 'What do you want?' Just like that. 'What do you want?' Then she said 'What do you *want*?' Like that. Louder. Like whoever it was didn't answer her the first time. Boy, she was mad."

Florence paused for a cookie and Mrs. Huntemann took up the slack. "You see, Florence couldn't hear the other person. That Joyce was pretty loud, so she could hear her, but she couldn't hear whoever was with her. Right, Florence?"

"Oh, yes. She was loud." Florence reached for the last two cookies.

Mrs. Huntemann was in her element. She sat with both hands gripping her knees, like the last time I was here, her blue eyes as bright as her sapphire ring. "Well, go on Florence! Tell her what she said next."

Florence spoke with her mouth full, crumbs falling down the front of her dress. "The next thing I remember is her saying something like 'What about Angela?' At least I think it was Angela.... Then she listed off a bunch of other names I don't remember."

"Yes you do, you told me yesterday. That Joyce said, 'What about Angela?' Then she said, 'And Lillian?'—like she wanted to know what they thought, you know? And then she said, 'What about *Natalie*?'" Mrs. Huntemann's face was turning purple with excitement.

"Wait a minute!" Florence spat a few cookie crumbs onto Mrs. Huntemann's lap and poked a finger at her. "I remember now. She said, 'Why do you say that? Did *you* kill her?'"

"Right!" Mrs. Huntemann clapped her hands, "You see? *That Joyce knows who killed the little girl!* Tell her the rest, Florence."

155

"Well, I couldn't hear anything for a few minutes, so I moved a little closer to the door." She walked her fingers across her lap for effect. "Still couldn't hear the other person, though. I heard the woman say something like, 'I don't understand why you're here,' and then a little later, 'Why me?' Then, just when I thought I wasn't going to hear anything else, she said, 'Don't worry, everything you tell me is strictly confidential.'"

Finished, she sat back and licked a fingertip, tapping it against her chest to pick up the surviving crumbs.

Mrs. Huntemann looked at me expectantly. "Well? Didn't I tell you? That Joyce knows somethin'."

If only we could fill in the rest of the conversation. Then I remembered Robert's datebook. Apparently, when he met with Joyce as his book had indicated, he had admitted to killing Natalie.

Mrs. Huntemann still looked at me, waiting for me to respond. Florence eyed me skeptically, sucking her finger.

"I don't know what to say. I guess we should tell the police."

"Tell the police?" Mrs. Huntemann's brows shot up. "Tell 'em what? That Florence is an eavesdropper who spends half her time listenin' in on other people's conversations through their doors?"

Florence scowled.

"Well, Robert confessed—Joyce obviously hasn't told them, I think we should."

"Robert? You think it was him with that Joyce?"

"Yes, I saw his appointment book—he had a meeting with her on Tuesday at 4:30."

"Well, the time fits.... Florence, you think it was a man with that Joyce?"

"Sure do. Saw him come out about half an hour later."

Mrs. Huntemann's jaw fell open. "You never told me that! Why didn't you tell me that?"

"Dorothy Huntemann, I don't have to tell you everything. Just because I've known you since we were kids and you come fix me dinner every now and then doesn't mean I have to tell you every last thing that happens to me. Seems like you just expect me to go running around finding out everything that goes on just so you can have something to tell your other friends. Then you go and call me names right when I'm sitting here. I hate to think what you're saying about me behind my *back*."

"Oh, for goodness sake, Florence, I didn't either call you names."

"Did too. You called me an eavesdropper."

"Well I meant it as a compliment."

"Well all right."

With that, they both turned to me. I was amazed they could disagree so easily, and make up so quickly. Maybe if Carly and I were as honest with each other as Florence and Mrs. Huntemann were, I wouldn't be wondering now if I still had a best friend.

"So? Are you goin' to talk to that Joyce?"

"I—I guess I could.... But she's kind of hard to talk to. She doesn't reveal much. I doubt she'll tell me anything."

"Well, have to be persuasive, you do. Right, Florence? Like when I bought that microwave oven, remember? Got it home and cleared off a space for it on the counter—which wasn't easy, mind you, those things take up a lot of room. Had to put my mixer under the sink, I did. So I plugged it in and put a cup of water inside, like they tell you to, and *nothin'!* Must have left it in there a good fifteen minutes. Took it out, not even warm. So I called the store and they sent someone out, but he couldn't fix it. So I says to him 'Well, you just take it back and get me a new one.'"

Mrs. Huntemann set her chin firmly. I waited, but she didn't continue.

"And?"

"And they brought me a new one. Works fine. Used it to steam the asparagus tonight. You just have to be firm, that's all."

We talked for a few minutes longer, until Florence dozed off and Tinkerbell appeared on the couch behind her. Mrs. Huntemann intervened before the cat could make off with Florence's hair.

"Emma honey, hope you don't mind, but I told Florence you'd take her home. I'd take her myself, but the last time I drove at night I wound up in Baltimore. Think I took a wrong turn near by the expressway where they're buildin' that mini-mall...."

We said good-bye and I led Florence down the walk toward my car. The Norman Rockwell family in Natalie's house had closed their drapes, but the windows were still open. Music floated through the screen and I heard muted laughter as we passed. I glanced up at Natalie's window, imaging their little girl asleep somewhere behind it. I shuddered, suddenly afraid for her. Once I'd thought Natalie's family was perfect, too.

Florence chatted amiably as we walked up the drive, bringing me up to date on the plot of *All My Children*. I didn't recognize most of the names anymore, but concentrating on Florence's spirited narration made me forget about Robert for a while.

* * * * *

I walked with Florence all the way up to her apartment, hoping no one on the seventh floor was trying to sleep. She was railing on at full volume about a soap opera character who reminded her of one of her nieces. Apparently, Florence had serious doubts about both. At her door, Florence invited me in for a snack, but I declined, impressed with—and not a little envious of—her limitless appetite.

Turning around, I headed back down the hall at a good pace, acutely aware of the engraved plate on Joyce Slocombe's office door. I passed it without incident, letting out a slow breath, and pressed for the elevator. When it opened, she stepped out in front of me.

"Why, Emma! How nice to see you again." She glanced up the hall. "Did you want to see me?"

I watched helplessly as the elevator doors closed behind her.

"No, I, uh.... I was dropping a friend off."

"Oh, I see." She studied me for a moment. "How are you?"

Her voice took on that velvet sincerity I'd been so drawn to just a few days ago. Now it cut through me like a razor blade. "I'm fine."

"I see.... Would you like to come in for some coffee?"

My eyes flew to the 'down' button, and I knew I couldn't face her tonight.

"Um, no, I can't. I have to get home. I have.... I'm expecting a call."

She looked at me, her head tilted, her fingers curled around the long thin strap of her purse. "Are you sure? We could talk...."

"No. I mean, yes. I...." I took a deep breath. "I do have something I want to talk to you about. But not now. Tomorrow."

Joyce studied me, sliding a thumb thoughtfully up and down the purse strap. "Why don't you come by around ten-thirty. I'm free for half an hour or so. Is that all right?"

I pressed the down arrow and nodded, feeling something constrict around my throat.

"I'll see you tomorrow then. Take care of yourself, Emma."

The elevator arrived and I stepped inside, focusing at once on the numbers above the door. Joyce watched me from the hall until the doors closed.

Chapter 20

A friend of mine once recommended taking a Benadryl anti-histamine if you can't sleep. Whatever you do, don't take four.

I woke up Saturday morning to find my brain had petrified sometime during the night. It weighed in at a tad over three hundred pounds. In addition, my tongue had swollen to six times its normal size. My eyes were sealed shut. If thirty thousand eight-year-olds hadn't scheduled today for their Annual Pool Party and Scream-a-Thon just ten floors below my open window, I'm sure I could have slipped gently into a coma and never faced reality again.

Behind my glued eyelids, grisly scenes played themselves out in my head. My imagination took hold of what Florence had told me and twisted it, giving Natalie's and Robert's faces deep shadows and using the screams of the children outside to punctuate the storyline. Like in one of the hideous horror movies I'd gone to in high school, I saw Natalie die a hundred different ways, each more excruciating than the last. I saw her face under water, held beneath the surface by Robert's manicured hand. Above, children laughed and pointed, until something else drew their attention away. Then Natalie died. Alone, submerged, silent.

Gasping for air, I jerked up in bed. Robert. Natalie. Murder. Why? Last night, I'd driven myself to drug abuse trying to figure it out, but it still didn't make any sense. I concentrated on the facts. What did the cops look for when singling out a suspect?

160

Means, opportunity, motive.

Well, Robert had the means. According to the *Post,* the coroner was speculating Natalie had been suffocated with a pillow. Plenty of pillows around. I threw mine to the floor.

Opportunity. From what I remembered, Angela had been out the night Natalie disappeared, coming back around 10:30 after Natalie had gone to bed. Robert was there all night.

Motive.

I was right back where I started. A piece of the puzzle was missing. It hovered somewhere in the elusive periphery of my mind. And how did Bobbie figure into all this?

I considered taking four more Benadryl and leaving the rest to fate, but then I remembered my appointment with Joyce.

It was five minutes after ten. If I hurried, I could just make it.

* * * * *

Joyce set a steaming cup of cinnamon-scented coffee in front of me and I sucked down half of it, hoping the caffeine would give me courage. I needed answers.

"So what can I do for you Emma?"

"I want to know why Robert Campbell killed Natalie and what you're going to do about it."

Joyce only raised an eyebrow. "I see. Can you tell me why you think Robert is guilty?"

"Oh, come off it, Joyce. He told you himself. Someone overheard you. I just want to know why." I didn't know where my sudden courage was coming from, but I didn't stop to question it.

Joyce, her eyes soft and glistening, leaned forward. "Emma, I'm not sure I understand what you're saying. Can you start from the beginning? What makes you think I spoke with Robert?"

I was getting hot, my hands shaking. I pressed them together in my lap and watched as my knuckles turned white. "Someone heard you talking to him. You asked him if he killed Natalie and then you told him you'd keep it confidential." I looked at her.

161

"Why? Why won't you tell the police?"

She ignored my question. "When did this 'someone' say I met with Robert?"

"Tuesday afternoon. And I saw his datebook. I know you had an appointment with him at four-thirty."

"Four-thirty. I see." She sat back, caressing her mug, deep in thought. "Emma, why is it important to you to find out what happened to Natalie?"

I swallowed hard. "She was my best friend. I loved her. I have to know."

As Joyce watched me, my eyes locked again on the woman-orchid shimmering above her shoulder. The sensuous lines seemed to draw me in, swirling and pulling me down into the heart of the flower. The heart of the woman. Wet heat flowed through me, bringing my toes to life, then curled back up my legs and spine through my neck to my face. Soon it was running down my cheeks.

I was crying.

"Can you tell me what you're feeling?"

I sobbed. I couldn't stop. Natalie was gone, and so was Judy. Carly soon would be. Leaving me completely alone. I couldn't trust anyone. No one cared. Natalie was dead and no one cared.

Tissues materialized before me, and I clutched several in both hands, soaking them thoroughly. I couldn't breathe, I couldn't see. Everything hurt. My skin hurt, my eyes hurt, my soul hurt. I shredded the damp paper helplessly, wanting desperately to lie down and go to sleep. To avoid the pain.

Joyce didn't interrupt. Eventually I found my voice again. "It's just...I just feel so alone. I miss Natalie so much. I miss all of them so much...."

I started crying again, and soon I was pouring out most of my life story. My father. My grandfather. My mother. My childhood. College. Eric, Judy, Carly. Natalie. Everything. She listened closely, nodding and reaching out to me almost physically with her eyes. More than anything, I wanted to feel her arms around

162

me. I had to struggle to keep from going to her and falling into her lap.

I don't know how long I talked. When I finally slowed down, my throat was sore and my voice cracked as if I'd been screaming for hours.

Joyce waited till she was sure I had nothing more to say. "You're feeling a lot of very strong emotions right now. Fear, abandonment, betrayal. It goes back a long way."

I nodded. I felt embarrassed, vulnerable, but curiously, free and relieved. My arms seemed lighter, my head almost weightless. As if my whole body had heaved one long sigh.

"I'd like to help you sort through your feelings, Emma. Would you consider coming here once a week?"

I thought immediately of Carly and how she'd react. Then Kate's voice came into my mind. I considered how calm I felt now, how nice it was to have someone who actually listened. I nodded.

Hope seemed to dawn in my mind. Joyce gave me her card and I made an appointment for the following Wednesday.

Then I reminded her, "You haven't answered my questions about last Tuesday yet."

Joyce seemed pleased by my confidence. "Emma, I can't tell you who I was talking to or what they said, but I want to assure you, I'm not trying to hide anything from you or the police. I hope you know that."

"But you do know something."

Joyce paused and fiddled with her pen, tapping it lightly in her palm. "Emma, I'm very concerned about this. I'm constrained in what help I can offer you, but I do want to help. I'm going to try. Do you understand?"

I looked at her. She obviously had something in mind, but wouldn't reveal it to me. I realized there was nothing I could do but wait.

* * * * *

I'd promised my mother I'd go shopping with her, so at two-thirty I found myself reluctantly following her sprightly form through the mall.

We toured Macy's lingerie department, Mom picking through the bras and occasionally asking my opinion of certain styles.

"It is beyond me why something that requires only a few inches of fabric and a couple of eye-hooks costs thirty-six dollars. Oh for God's sake, will you look at this?"

She held up a bright red bra made of lace with black trim. Inserting her fingers, she separated the cups where the bra had been designed to reveal a woman's nipples. In spite of myself, I found it remarkably sexy.

"Can you imagine?" She replaced it, rolling her eyes, and headed for a rack of beige underwear, checking the tags for her size.

"Mom?"

"Yes, sweetheart. Do you see any thirty-four B's?"

I pulled one from the rack and handed it to her. She pressed it to her chest and viewed herself in a mirror on the wall.

"I wanted to talk to you about something."

"Sure, honey. What is it?"

She turned to me, still holding the bra against her dark blue sweatshirt.

"I've been thinking...about Natalie and everything."

Mom folded the bra and hanger over her arm and touched my cheek, brushing hair out of my face.

"Oh, honey, I wish you wouldn't get so upset about this."

"I know. I just...I can't help it."

Tears came to my eyes and Mom ushered me into a fitting room, sitting me down the low stool and pulling a tissue from her purse.

"What is it, honey?"

I told her about Carly and our argument, about Mrs. Huntemann pressuring me to find 'who did it,' and about the screw-up at work. She listened, wiping my eyes and holding my hand.

"I've decided to see someone. A therapist."

164

Mom's hand stiffened in mine.

She released it and stood, busying herself with trying on the bra. "I'm not sure I understand, Emma. Is this just about Natalie?"

I watched her in the mirror, thinking how familiar this scene was. Me behind her, meeting her eyes only in the safety of the glass.

"No, Mom. It's a lot of things. I talked to her this morning and it really helped."

Mom took off the bra and put her shirt back on, concentrating on getting the straps of the new bra back into their slots on the hanger.

"Do you think it's a bad idea?" I put a hand on her elbow, wishing she would look directly at me.

She turned and met my eyes. She looked ready to cry.

"Mom? What's wrong?"

"Did I do something, Emma? Was I a bad mother?"

I stood and took her in my arms, tears brimming in my own eyes.

"No, Mom, of course not. Why do you think that?"

She held me closely, burying her face in my shoulder. "I don't know. You just hear about therapists and they blame everything on the mother...I tried, Emma, I tried so hard. I always wanted the best for you. I'm sure I made a lot of mistakes, probably at times when I just didn't know what else to do, how to protect you...."

I patted her hair, trying to assure her that wasn't the case. Suddenly I froze.

Mom pulled away. "What is it Emma? Please, tell me."

She was panicking. I took her hand. "I just thought of something. About Natalie. God, why didn't I see it before? Mom, I have to go, okay? I swear, it's nothing to do with you. I love you, Mom. I love you so much."

* * * * *

165

It was nearly four when I got home. I had to reach Bobbie. My answering machine was blinking and I hit the rewind, hoping it was Carly.

"Emma, this is Bobbie Campbell. We need to talk. Meet me tonight at Cymbidium, seven o'clock."

She sounded angry. I didn't need to wonder how she got my number. Joyce Slocombe. It had been Bobbie in her office on Tuesday. Florence had mistaken her for a man, the same as she'd done with me when she first saw me. I'd been right all along. Bobbie was the key.

* * * * *

The cafe smelled of garlic and sweet basil. I stood in the entry scanning the crowd, but didn't see Bobbie.

"Hey Emma, good to see you again!" Sherry led me to a table upstairs, overlooking the street. I asked her to let Bobbie know where I was when she came in, and set my chair so I could see out the window. I scanned the street, nervously watching for Bobbie.

She slid in across from me at exactly seven o'clock. She wore a deep green camp shirt and jeans, her skin bronzed and glowing. Her hair was slightly mussed, giving her a wind-blown, outdoors look. In her right hand, she held a brass keychain in the shape of a lambda. She absentmindedly stroked and polished the metal with her thumb.

"I'm going to be honest with you, Emma. At first, I was glad to see you. Very glad. But now you're getting too close. I want you out of this."

It surprised me that Bobbie was so angry. Her nostrils flared slightly when she spoke, and her shoulders hunched with tension. It hurt to have such animosity coming from her. I remembered the electric feel of her fingertips sliding past mine, the strength of her eyes drawing me in. Now they were leveled in cold challenge, her arms folded on the table like a barricade.

"I just want to help, Bobbie. Natalie was my best friend."

166

Bobbie's eyes narrowed and a muscle in her cheek began to twitch. "I don't need your help. I can handle this myself, all right?"

Despite her hostility, I knew I had to tell her what I suspected. Maybe then she'd change her mind. "Bobbie, I loved Natalie. This whole thing is killing me. I can't let it go." I looked into her eyes, meeting her hooded gaze. "I've found something out. Something important...and awful."

I faltered. This was so hard. She waited, nothing softening in her face.

"I think...I think Natalie was being sexually abused. By your father."

Bobbie's eyes widened.

"Joyce Slocombe told me. She tried to counsel Natalie, but she wouldn't talk."

Bobbie spoke in a rush of anger. "Natalie's dead, there's nothing you can do for her anymore. Just go home to your memories. You have them. I *don't*."

Tears threatened in her eyes. Until now, I hadn't thought about how she must feel. Bobbie had been only four when Natalie died. I reached out to her. "Do you remember her at all?"

Bobbie seemed to cave in, her shoulders falling and the lines of her face giving way. "No, I don't. After she disappeared, Angela destroyed all the pictures of her that had been hanging on the walls. I kept one of both of us sitting on a blanket at a picnic. I wore it out looking at it every night. Eventually it just disintegrated. Later on I invented a face and a personality for her. I used to write her letters and have conversations with her when there was no one else around. Somehow, I thought if I kept her memory alive, she'd come back."

So I wasn't the only one. I touched her hand and she didn't flinch. "I know what you mean. When I found out she was dead, I realized I couldn't remember her very well. But I wanted to, to remember everything we'd done. And now it's all coming back." I tried to make her smile. "At least I don't have to look at that picture of her on the news anymore."

"I cut it out of the paper. I felt like it was all I had left of her." Bobbie contemplated me with her chocolate eyes. The setting sun outside the window reflected in them, the golden specks dancing like fire. Rays of light twisted through her hair, smoldering red at the ends. She looked so much like Natalie.

Bobbie bit her lower lip and looked out the window. Her pain seemed to fill the air between us. I wished I could take her in my arms.

She faced me again, with determination, but without anger.

"Just stay out of this now. This is my problem, I'll deal with it."

"How?"

She rose and turned to go.

"Watch the news."

Chapter 21

I stayed at the table, watching Bobbie walk the length of the sidewalk toward her car. She glanced up at me as she climbed in, almost as if saying good-bye, then drove off in the direction of the parkway.

Watch the news. I stirred my iced tea with a long spoon, worrying about what Bobbie was going to do. I didn't think she believed my accusation of Robert—her reaction had been strange. Almost as if she'd already known.

Marie approached, flipping through the pages of her notepad and pulling a pencil from her back pocket.

"You ready? I saw Athena there high-tail it out of here. Weird. She wished me a 'good life.' What'd she do, enlist?"

Suddenly, the last pieces of the puzzle fell into place. Images, fragments of things I'd heard and seen, rushed before my eyes, resolving into one clear, terrifying picture.

I slapped a few dollar bills into Marie's hand and ran down the stairs to my car. Bobbie had been headed toward the Campbell's house. If I broke a few traffic laws, maybe I could get there in time.

* * * * *

I tucked the Celica under cover of the oleander. The courtyard was deserted. Bobbie's Honda was parked by the front door. Robert's BMW was nowhere in sight.

Two screened sections of the huge picture window were open and, as I walked toward the house, I could hear Bobbie's raised voice. I crept alongside the house and knelt beneath the window, looking through a slit in the living room drapes.

Bobbie was standing in front of the long mirror, her arms spread, tears running down her face.

"Don't you get it? He *killed* her. We can't let him get away with it."

Avoiding the brambles behind me, I shifted my position to try and see who Bobbie was talking to. Lillian Campbell sat primly in a wing back chair.

"Barbara, calm down. We'll solve nothing with you hurling these ridiculous accusations at the top of your voice."

I found a point from which I could see Bobbie clearly and also Lillian's reflection in the mirror behind her. The low line of evergreen shrubs framing the window provided some cover, but I knew my head and shoulders would be visible from the driveway if anyone approached. I crossed my fingers that the Campbells had dismissed their armed guards.

"You've been willing to cover up Natalie's murder from the start, Grandmother. I know you're trying to get Senator Randolph to force an indictment against Frank Mercer. Don't you give a damn that he's innocent? That *your own son* murdered your granddaughter?"

Lillian's voice cut like a knife. "Natalie was *not* my granddaughter. And you have no proof whatsoever that your father killed her."

"Listen to you! Just because your precious blue Campbell blood didn't flow in my sister's veins, you think you have no responsibility to find her true killer?" Bobbie screamed in frustration, stomping in front of the mirror and flinging her hands about.

"Barbara, sit down. I mean it. Your father will be home any moment, and I will not have him walk in and see you like this."

"I don't give a *fuck* how he sees me!"

"Barbara!"

Bobbie stopped moving and turned to face Lillian. She lowered her voice, speaking deliberately.

"Read my lips, Grandmother. *Robert Campbell is a child molester*. He sexually abused me from the time I was born until I turned sixteen. He only stopped because I told him I'd kill him if he ever did it again."

"That is enough. I will not listen to this any longer."

Lillian turned toward the window; I ducked out of sight. When I raised my head again, I had a different view of the room and could see past Bobbie into the foyer. Angela was standing outside the archway leading into the room, hidden from Lillian's view. She had on a long white nightgown and hugged her bare arms close to her chest. She didn't move.

I had to get inside. I thought about knocking, but Angela was right by the front door. She'd answer, and I had to get to Bobbie first.

I slipped beneath the window, then ran past the front door and around the side of the house. A narrow path ran above the wide expanse of lawn that led down to the birch trees. I knew the den was on my right. I crossed my fingers one of the windows was open.

The light was fading quickly. The house blocked the sun's waning rays, and no light came from the den. The windows were about five feet off the ground. I squeezed between two large bushes and peeked in through the first window I came to. The den was empty. The window was closed, but I pushed the screen against the glass and it slid upward easily. After prying the screen loose, I used it as a brace to lift the window farther up the sash. Throwing the screen on the grass, I put my foot on the head of a spigot set into the wall and hoisted myself inside.

The banker's lamp on the desk had been left on and I saw Bobbie's keys laying in the small pool of light. As I glanced around, I saw a stack of brand-new law books by the desk, some lesbian novels in the book shelf and Bobbie's college diploma framed on the wall by the door. I had just assumed this room was Robert's, so I hadn't seen the obvious evidence that Bobbie laid claim to it. Bobbie's room. Somehow I felt safer knowing that.

Thick carpeting muffled my footsteps, and I pressed my ear against the cool wood of the door. Then I turned the doorknob slowly.

Peering through the tiny crack, I saw Angela in the foyer, her back to the wall. She was facing me now, her eyes closed, listening to the argument between Bobbie and Lillian in the living room.

"God damn it! I can't believe you're defending him! Even if you don't give a damn about Natalie, I *am* your granddaughter—don't you care at all what he did to me?"

"Of course I do, Barbara, but it's not as if he hurt you physically. I'm sure he meant no harm. Perhaps you're taking it the wrong way."

Bobbie spoke through tears, years of pain coming through in her voice. I ached for her, my chest tightening with every word. "He would come into the bathroom when I was taking a bath and...touch me. He fondled my breasts when I practiced the piano. He made me touch his penis.... How was I supposed to take that? Tell me, Grandma. *How is that not supposed to hurt me?*"

Angela opened her eyes. She showed no reaction to what Bobbie was saying. Incredibly, she turned and walked slowly up the stairs.

When she was safely out of sight, I crossed the foyer into the archway. Bobbie and Lillian were sitting close on the couch, Lillian patting Bobbie's knee.

"Barbara, you must try to look at this from your father's point of view. He's a very powerful man, but he has his weaknesses. You mustn't blame him for loving you and trying to show that love. I'm sure he was just trying to show how much he cares about you."

I shuddered at Lillian's repellent logic. Bobbie pulled away from her touch. Then she saw me, and her eyes grew wide.

"Emma! What are you doing here?"

"Bobbie, I have to talk to you—"

Lillian glared at me, pulling Bobbie toward her by the arm. "Emma, I don't know how you got in here but I insist you leave immediately."

"No, Mrs. Campbell. I have to talk to her."

Bobbie broke free of Lillian's grasp and came to me, wiping her eyes. "Emma, I told you I can handle this. It's all out in the open now. He's not going to do it anymore."

"Bobbie, you're wrong. You have to listen to me. Angela told me...I think—"

Bobbie's eyes flicked over my shoulder and I turned to see Angela framed in the archway. She had put on a flowing white silk bathrobe over her nightgown, her blonde hair cascading down her shoulders. The long, wide sleeves of the robe fanned out around her like angel's wings. The effect was beatific, except for the gun in her right hand.

I instinctively pulled Bobbie behind me and backed away, noticing Lillian had frozen on the couch.

"Angela, what on earth—?"

"Don't worry, Lillian. It's not too late. Bobbie's right, it's all out in the open now. But it doesn't have to be. It doesn't ever have to leave this room."

She stared at Bobbie, and something glimmered in her eyes, a decision she'd made. And something else I couldn't define. She held the gun loosely in her hand, and I forced myself to concentrate on how to get it away from her.

Angela addressed Bobbie as if I wasn't there. "I knew what Robert was doing to Natalie. She told me. But it was too late. I'd already married him. I wanted to protect her, I tried everything I could think of, but he didn't stop. There was nothing else I could do."

She'd said the same thing to me last Saturday as she stared out the window, tears rolling down her face. And today my own mother had said these words in Macy's, but I'd heard the critical difference. Only one had confessed to murder.

"Angela, please. You can't get away with this. For God's sake put the gun down."

She looked at me for the first time. "Emma? What are you doing here? You should be in bed, sweetheart, it's late. Your mother must be worried."

Bobbie gasped. Lillian sat stockstill on the couch, her eyes locked on the gun. I gauged that if I backed Bobbie up as far as the fireplace, and drew Angela farther into the room, Lillian could get behind her. Or at least slip out and call the police. But Lillian wouldn't meet my eyes.

"Momma?" Bobbie's voice broke behind me. "Momma, why? You loved Natalie. How could you kill her?"

"I had to protect her. I couldn't let him do that to her anymore. She was so afraid. She said to me over and over, 'Make him stop, Mommie, please, make him stop.' But he didn't. There was nothing else I could do."

I began to move ever so slowly backward, pushing Bobbie with me. I searched the room for something to throw at the gun, but there was nothing but the brass lioness underneath the coffee table, and it looked like it weighed a ton. Besides, I couldn't move away from Bobbie.

"I miss her, you know." Angela's eyes clouded, but the gun was steady in her hand. "She used to come to me at night. Her spirit—she seemed finally happy. He couldn't touch her anymore or make her do those awful things. But since they found her, she hasn't been back."

Lillian's jaw dropped and she pulled her knees in tighter, her hand over her heart. I gave up hoping she could help disarm Angela. It was up to me now.

"I thought she would be safe there, at the terrace. That's what she called it, you know. It was her secret hiding place. You remember, Emma, she loved it there. She was so happy climbing around those steps, wasn't she?"

"Yes, she was."

I decided to keep her talking, hoping she'd forget about the gun. "We used to go there all the time. It was our fort."

"Yes, of course, the fort. I wanted to put her there, but it was so high. I couldn't see in the dark. I couldn't climb up with her in my arms. And she was so cold."

When she stopped talking, I prodded her on. "Why did you decide to save her that night?"

"Because she couldn't sleep. I came home and went up to tuck her in, but she was wide awake. She was sitting up, with the window open and all the lights on. I tucked her back into bed, and she told me why she couldn't sleep. She said he came in again while I was out. He touched her and he told her it was because I was away. So she was waiting for me to get back so he wouldn't touch her anymore. After awhile she went to sleep. She looked so beautiful when she was asleep. So peaceful. Her hand curled around mine."

Angela put a hand on her wrist, remembering. The gun hung from her other hand in menacing counterpoint to the tender memory.

"I just wanted her to stay that way forever. Safe. You understand that, don't you Bobbie?"

Bobbie was crying silently. Her hand gripping my arm trembled.

"No, Momma, I don't. Why didn't you just leave him?"

Angela looked at her daughter with a puzzled frown.

"Leave him? I couldn't do that. He was my husband."

"And Natalie was your *daughter*, but you killed her! What about me, Momma? Why didn't you kill me?" Bobbie screamed in frustration, trying to get around me. But I blocked her way.

On the couch, Lillian suddenly turned to the window. A car was pulling up in the driveway. Angela was staring at Bobbie, and I didn't think she heard it. I listened to the car door slam and footsteps approach the front door. An eternity later, Robert walked through the door and came into the living room behind Angela.

"Bobbie, I told you to park your car off to the side. It's right in the middle of the—What's going on, here? Angela?"

Angela turned to him, the gun still raised. He took a step backward, his eyes bulging.

"Angela, Jesus Christ, put that down!"

"Robert? Robert, why? I gave you Bobbie, why wasn't she enough?"

He stared at her wildly, uncomprehending.

"What do you mean? What are you talking about?"

"I gave you Bobbie. But you still had to hurt Natalie. Why?"

I saw Angela's face reflected in the mirror. Tears came to her eyes as she faced Robert for the first time.

"What do you mean you 'gave me Bobbie'? What is this all about?" He made a move and Angela motioned with the gun. He froze.

"I knew, Robert. I knew all along. I couldn't understand why you had to touch her, but she told me all about it. So I gave you Bobbie. I thought if you had your own little girl, you'd stop hurting mine. But you didn't. Why, Robert? Why didn't you stop?"

Fear dawned in Robert's eyes. "Angela, listen to me. I didn't hurt her. It was Frank. Right, Mother? Frank killed her. Please, Angela, you've got to believe me. Mother, tell her I'm right!"

When Lillian moved, Angela turned slightly, the gun still pointed at Robert.

"Frank. Frank knew. Natalie told him, too. But he got angry. He told her he'd take her away from me. She was afraid of him. She didn't want to leave me. That night, that awful night, I told him I'd protect her. He didn't believe me. He does now."

Robert's eyes grew even wider as he realized what Angela had done.

"My God, Angela. You? You killed Natalie?"

She took a step toward her husband. Her voice lost its wondering, ethereal quality. She was discovering the truth in front of our eyes. "No, Robert. You did. You killed her innocence. Her trust. She wasn't my little girl anymore. She was afraid, confused, alone. I used to come into her room and find her touching herself. She poked holes in her dolls between the legs so she could stick things up inside them. You taught her that, Robert. You killed my baby."

"Angela, listen to me. I was just trying to...I never meant to hurt her. Bobbie? You know I never meant to hurt you girls, don't you?"

Bobbie managed to step around me. "It doesn't matter what you meant to do. You *did* hurt me. And you *did* hurt Natalie. It's unforgivable, Daddy."

Lillian stood up and moved toward Angela. "I've heard enough of this!" Robert lunged forward and grabbed the gun, twisting Angela's arm downward. As they struggled, the gun disappeared between them. Robert's arms closed around Angela, and she fought to break free. When Bobbie tried to get to them, I held her back with all my strength.

Then the gun went off.

Chapter 22

Lillian screamed as Robert fell heavily to the ground, curling into a ball at Angela's feet. Angela still held the gun in both hands, the barrel pointed down at him. She turned her face to me.

"Emma?"

I walked toward her slowly, gesturing to Bobbie to hold back.

"I'm here, Angela. It's all right. Give me the gun."

She looked down at the gun as if she'd never seen it before. She raised it slowly, meeting my eyes. She looked completely lost, as if she'd just awakened from a deep sleep.

I closed my hand around the gun barrel and soon its full weight lay in my hands. I'd never held a gun before. I took it by the handle and gingerly passed it to Bobbie, who'd moved up behind me.

Robert moaned on the floor, his hands clutching his groin. Blood stained his suit and began to soak into the carpet. Lillian rushed over and fell on him, cradling his head in her lap and crying uncontrollably. Angela watched in wonder as blood began to soak the hem of her bathrobe, the fabric acting like a blotter and spreading the stain quickly upward.

I took her arm and led her to the wing chair, facing away from the grisly scene in the entry. Bobbie had slipped out and I could hear her calm, reasoned voice coming from the den, calling for an ambulance and the police.

Angela focused on the coffee table, her eyes glazing over and her hands resting limply in her lap. She was transfixed, reading something unseen in the table's watery depths. I went back to Lillian and Robert under the arch. Sirens were already approaching the house.

"Oh, God. Oh, God. Please don't take him. Please, God, please." Lillian sobbed, rocking back and forth, petting Robert's flushed face. His slick, handsome features were contorted with pain.

Bobbie stood motionless in the foyer, staring at Robert sprawled on the floor in his own blood. I stepped over him and went to her, pulling her face toward me.

"Bobbie? Are you all right?"

"I don't know, Em. I don't know."

I led her into the den and seated her in a chair, wrapping her with a quilt from the hearth. I knew she was in shock, but before I left the room, she took my hand and looked into my eyes. I saw the future in them.

Commotion in the hall told me the police and paramedics had arrived. I closed the den doors behind me in time to see Robert being wheeled away on a stretcher to a waiting ambulance, it's bright red and white lights blazing in the courtyard. Lillian followed, holding his hand and demanding he be taken to Georgetown University Hospital.

Angela still sat in the wing chair, her thoughts locked beyond the present. A uniformed police officer tried to talk to her. "Ma'am? Please, ma'am, I need some information." He looked up, bewildered, as I walked in.

"I can help you." I gave him all the details I could, and he took copious notes, whistling in amazement a few times. I knew that by telling everything that had happened, I had committed Bobbie to revealing her victimization to the police, maybe even the public, but I felt it was the right decision. After all, she hadn't been at fault.

I assured the officer that Bobbie would be down tomorrow to make a statement. He told me he'd have to take Angela into custody and admit her to the County Hospital mental health ward for the night.

As the door closed behind them, I took a long, deep breath. The blood on the Campbells' snow white carpet was turning black. I wondered vaguely who would clean it up. I didn't think it was possible now.

* * * * *

Bobbie had turned on the gas fireplace and was watching the flames when I entered. She smiled up at me and I sat in the chair beside her, noticing that the color had returned to her cheeks.

"I love this room. Angela had it decorated for him, but he never used it, so I moved in. I feel safe here." She laughed sadly. "It's the only room in the house besides their bedroom that has a lock on the door."

I reached over and took her hand. It was warm in mine. She looked at me, puzzled. "How did you know, Emma? How did you know it was Angela?"

I shrugged. "She said the same thing to me last Saturday that she said to you tonight. That there was 'nothing *else* she could do.' But I didn't realize what it meant till today."

We sat in silence, Bobbie studying the flames. Occasionally a tear rolled down her cheek.

"Bobbie, I'm sorry how this all came down. But I don't think Angela meant she didn't love you...I think she didn't know what she was saying."

Bobbie sighed, and her whole body shook. "I've always known she didn't really want any part of me. I thought it was because she'd lost Natalie, you know? That she was afraid to love another little girl. Eventually I realized she couldn't love me, but I never knew why. Maybe because of my father and what it made me.... I suppose that's when I started calling her Angela. 'Momma' seemed too...personal."

Bobbie closed her eyes and new tears fell down her cheeks.

180

"You're not alone, Bobbie. I'm here and I'm not leaving." I could see a deep, old fear behind her eyes. A fear I recognized.

"Joyce said I could trust you. At the funeral, she said I should talk to you. That maybe you could help me. We argued about it afterward. I got so mad when I saw you in here, in my room. I just felt like you were invading every part of my life."

I was glad we were holding hands. "I felt the same way about you at first. I thought you were going to take Natalie away from me. My memories of her. I don't know. It doesn't make any sense now."

"I should have listened to Joyce. I did try to call you once, but when I got your machine, I just couldn't speak. I didn't know what to say without telling you...what he did to me." She bowed her head, tears splashing onto the arm of the leather chair.

"Bobbie, look at me. It wasn't your fault. None of this was your fault. Not Robert's abuse. Not Angela's crimes. Not Natalie's death. None of it."

Bobbie looked at me, slowly a spark or two glimmered in the flecks in her eyes.

"Can I ask you something, Emma?"

"Anything."

"What was she like?"

I saw that future again in her eyes, felt it safe and warm as all those special hours in my childhood fort.

Bobbie moved closer. "Natalie. What was she like?"

I took a deep breath and stared into the fire.

This was going to take awhile.

Epilogue

Ring...Ring...Ring....

"Hi! It's me. Leave a message!" *Beeeeeeeeeep.*

"Hey, you—where are you? It's one in the morning. And I thought I was the wild one.... Guess what? I have a surprise for you, but I'm not revealing anything on the phone. You're just gonna have to call me.... So, call me, OK? I have to tell you what happened with San Francisco, the assholes. You're not gonna believe this, but they said I was overqualified. I blame you, of course. If you hadn't axed all the typos from my resumé, I'd be partying it up in the City by the Bay right now. So you owe me dinner. *Out..*" Carly laughed, half-heartedly.

"Em? Are you there? Listen, I'm sorry about the other night. Call me and we'll get together and eat and talk and cry and whatever else you want to do. You can let me know how your investigation is going...I miss you. Call me when you get in, OK? Doesn't matter how late. I'm always here." *Beeeeeeeeeep.*

AUTHOR'S NOTE

Unlike Natalie, I survived the abuse, but a part of me died at a very young age. I also shut out perhaps the one person I needed the most, my sister. This book is dedicated to her because, thankfully, I still have the chance to tell my best friend I love her.

* * * * *

Of course, there are other people in my life who deserve to see their names in print—I'd put them in lights, if I could.

To Jacqueline DiMauro, who nourishes my body, my mind and my heart: I love you and the dog you rode in on. Always.

To Rita Cortes, without whom this book would still be a nagging buzz in my brain: Thanks for your patience, your confidence and your love. It's nice knowing you're always there.

And to Vivien Deitz: Sometimes, as I watch you caring your way out of a job, I can't help wishing we never had to stop.

ABOUT THE AUTHOR

When she isn't watching television, Jessica Lauren writes junk mail for a publishing company. A proud graduate of Rice University, Jessica grew up in the suburbs of California and now lives in Arlington, Virginia—alone, because her apartment building doesn't allow cats.

Otherbooks from New Victoria

Mystery-Adventure

Woman with Red Hair—Brunel—The mystery of her mother's death takes Magalie into the swamps and the slums of France, her only clue the memory of a woman with red hair. ISBN 0-934678-30-8 ($8.95)

Death by the Riverside—Redmann—Detective Mickey Knight finds herself slugging through thugs and slogging through swamps to expose a dangerous drug ring. ISBN 0-934678-27-8 ($8.95)

Mysteries by Sarah Dreher

A Captive In Time—Stoner finds herself inexplicably transported to a small town in the Colorado Territory, time 1871. When, if ever, will she find a phone to call home? ISBN 0-934678-22-7 ($9.95)

Stoner McTavish —The first Stoner mystery—Dream lover Gwen, in danger in the Grand Tetons. *"Sensitive, funny and unabashedly sweet, Stoner McTavish is worth the read."* ($7.95) ISBN 0-934678-06-5

Something Shady— Stoner gets trapped in the clutches of the evil Dr. Millicent Tunes. *"The piece de resistance of the season...I think it's the funniest book I ever read."* ($8.95) ISBN 0-934678-07-3

Gray Magic— Stoner and Gwen head to Arizona, but a peaceful vacation turns frightening when Stoner becomes a combatant in the great struggle between the Hopi Spirits of good and evil. ($8.95) ISBN-0-934678-11-1

Adventure / Romance

Kite Maker— Van Auken—Melvina drives up to a women's bar in a spiffy new Cadillac convertible...and drives off with Sal , one of the mainstays of the community, in search of a long lost friend. ($8.95) ISBN 0-934678-32-4

Cody Angel—Whitfield—Dana struggles for self-esteem and love through her emotional entanglements— with her boss, with Frankie, a bike dyke, and Jerri, who enjoys sex as power. ISBN 0-934678-28-6 ($8.95)

In Unlikely Places—Beguin—While following a dream of exploring Africa, nineteenth century adventurer Lily Bascombe finds herself searching for the elusive Miss Margery Pool. ISBN 0-934578- 25-1 ($8.95)

Mari — Hilderley.—The story of the evolving relationship between Mari, an Argentinian political activist, and Judith, a New York City musician. ISBN-0-934678- 23-5 ($8.95)

Dark Horse— Lucas—Fed up with corruption in local politics, lesbian Sidney Garrett runs for mayor and falls in love with her socialite campaign worker. ISBN-0-934678--21-9 ($8.95)

As The Road Curves—Dean—Ramsey, with a reputation for never having to sleep alone, takes off from a prestigious lesbian magazine on an adventure of a lifetime. ISBN-0-934678-17-0 ($8.95)

All Out—Alguire—Winning a medal at the Olympics is Kay Strachan's all-consuming goal until a budding romance threatens her ability to go all out for the gold. ISBN-0-934678-16-2 ($8.95)

Look Under the Hawthorn—Frye—Stonedyke Edie Cafferty from Vermont searches for her long lost daughter and meets Anabelle, a jazz pianist looking for her birth mother. ISBN-0-934678-12-X ($7.95)

Runway at Eland Springs— Béguin—Flying supplies into the African bush, Anna gets herself into conflict with a game hunter, and finds love and support with Jilu, the woman at Eland Springs. ISBN-0-934678-10-3 ($7.95).

Promise of the Rose Stone —McKay—Mountain warrior Issa is banished to the women's compound in the living satellite where she and her lover Cleothe plan an escape with Cleothe's newborn baby. ISBN-0-934678-09-X ($7.95)

Humor

Cut Outs and Cut Ups A Fun'n Games Book for Lesbians—Dean, Wells, and Curran—Games, puzzles, astrology, paper dolls—an activity book for lesbians ISBN-0-934678-20-0 ($8.95)

Found Goddesses: Asphalta to Viscera—M. Grey &J.Penelope—*"Found Goddesses is wonderful. I've had more fun reading it than any book in the last two years."* —Joanna Russ. ISBN-0-934678-18-9 ($7.95)

Morgan Calabresé; The Movie—N. Dunlap- Wonderfully funny comic strips. Politics, relationships, and softball as seen through the eyes of Morgan Calabresé ISBN-0-934678-14-6 ($5.95)

Short Fiction/Plays

Secrets—Newman—The surfaces and secrets, the joys and sensuality and the conflicts of lesbian relationships are brought to life in these stories. ISBN 0-934678-24-3 ($8.95)

Lesbian Stages—"Sarah Dreher's plays are good yarns firmly centered in a Lesbian perspective with specific, complex, often contradictory (just like real people) characters." —Kate McDermott ($9.95)ISBN 0-934678-15-4

The Names of the Moons of Mars— Schwartz—In these stories the author writes humorously as well as poignantly about our lives as women and as lesbians. ISBN-0-934678-19-7 ($8.95).

Audiotape read by author from **The Names of the Moons of Mars** ($9.95) ISBN 0-934678-26-X

History

Radical Feminists of Heterodoxy— Schwarz—Numerous tantalizing photographs that accompany the warm lively narrative of the women and the times in which they lived. ISBN-0934678- 08-1   ($8.95)   —TheWomen's Studies Review

Available from your favorite bookstore or

Order directly from New Victoria Publishers, PO Box 27 Norwich, Vt. 05055